Being a Friend

Volume 2
of Memorial Service

Susan Larmon

To a friend indeed, Ann Whaley

*"A new city can change you,
in the way a friend can change you,
and there are moments in life
where both happen at once."*

The Bohemians
(by Jasmin Darznik)

Being a Friend

1

The minute she walked into the Asheville church, Amelia noticed the long line of people waiting to offer their condolences to a young man in his thirties who was standing near the coffin. She didn't recognize him, being so new to the parish herself, but she stopped to glance at the picture of the woman who had died – Mrs. Alice Clark, who could certainly have been the young man's mother. Although Amelia was running late to sing with the choir for the funeral, something about his obvious sadness touched her heart and made her join the line to speak to him.

"My name is Amelia Flynn." She extended her hand to him, and he took it with a questioning smile. "I'm new in town, but I'll be singing the funeral Mass with the choir. I'm so sorry for your loss."

"My mother would appreciate that so much, Amelia. Thank you…. I'm Phil Clark – do you live near here?"

"My husband and I live in West Asheville now."

"Really? So do I. You and your husband should stop by my house this afternoon – maybe we're neighbors! Then we can talk more, and I'll introduce you to all my friends who live nearby. Please come…."

"Thanks, Phil. I'll think about it, but now I must go and get ready for Mass."

"My address is in the program, Amelia. I hope I'll see you and your husband later, any time after 1 PM."

The church was quite full by the time Mass started, Amelia noted from the vantage point of the choir up front. There was a beautiful young woman sitting with Phil in the first row of pews. She must be his wife or girlfriend, Amelia guessed, judging from the way they interacted. Then, just before the homily, the pastor surprised everyone by calling on Phil's son to address the congregation. The thirteen-year-old timidly approached the microphone near the altar and began to speak.

"My Grandma Alice had trouble talking after her first stroke," he said, "and I gave her this journal so she could write down her thoughts. I'd like to read a short passage to you now." Derek opened the journal, and read slowly. "I want you all to celebrate my life, instead of mourning my death. I've had a long and happy life – due in no small part to the love of my late husband Daniel, my son Phil, and my grandson Derek. So remember, no tears when I am gone, or I will haunt your dreams until you find your smiles again. Live life to the fullest, as I have tried to do, and then you too will have no regrets."

Amelia was impressed by Derek's self-confidence in front of the congregation, and watched as he sat back down and Phil proudly put his arm around his son. A woman on the other side of Derek took his hand. Which one was his mother, Amelia wondered? Now she was really curious, and decided to accept Phil's invitation to the gathering at his house later. His street wasn't that far from theirs, as it turned out, and they needed to make some friends in their new community, anyway. She'd ask Jack about it when she got home.

—

Amelia told Jack about meeting Phil at his mother's funeral, and talked him into coming along with her. They could actually walk to Phil's house, which turned out to be a 1950s craft cottage in West Asheville. He had moved back in with his mother when she became ill, he told them, and now he had decided to stay on there.

Phil introduced them to the lovely girl who had sat next to him in church – Lorraine, whom he called his girlfriend. Then there was her older brother Jeff, who lived next door with his partner Eric. They were both teachers and seemed really nice.

But the real treat was meeting Phil's son Derek, who was there with his mother – Phil's ex-girlfriend Alicia. That solved *that* mystery! Derek talked about living in nearby Waynesville with his mother, except for occasional weekends here with his father. Alicia was very open about co-parenting with Phil, and Amelia had the feeling that she would like to get back together with Derek's father. Yikes! Her head was swimming with all the people they had met that afternoon, and who was related to whom! Time to go home and let Phil be alone with his family and friends – and his mother's spirit.

"Well, it's a start," Amelia smiled, as they walked home together.

"We're definitely not in Maryland anymore," Jack shook his head. He had resisted the idea of moving to North Carolina to retire, despite the beauty of the Blue Ridge Mountains.

"Do you think Loraine lives here with Phil? She said that she and her brother Jeff grew up right next door to Phil and his parents."

"How cozy. But I think she said she lives and works in Wilmington now.

"That's over near the Outer Banks, all the way to the east coast from here. It would be a full day's drive, but we should probably check it out sometime."

"That means a long-distance relationship for them – not the easiest kind to maintain."

"They're young – probably half our age. If it's meant to be, they'll manage it. Maybe he'll move over there with her…."

"I hope not," Amelia said. "Not when we've just made some new friends *here*."

—

It wasn't long before the reality of a newly-built house with a sizable mortgage and costly upkeep convinced Amelia and Jack that their dream of an early retirement might have been a bit premature. "We could always go back to work part-time," Jack kidded, but Amelia took him seriously.

"Why not? Maybe I could resurrect my teaching career, and you could find a way to get paid for talking."

"Very funny. In the meantime, let's go over to the Biltmore Estate in Asheville, and see what all the fuss is about." Everyone they met here had raved about George Vanderbilt's mansion in the mountains, completed in the early 1900s.

Vanderbilt had thought of it as a retreat for his family and friends from the hustle and bustle of New York City, and the pure mountain air as an antidote for their exhaust-filled lungs. Even now, the mansion was still the largest privately-owned house in the United States. Of course, it employed hundreds of tour guides, restaurant workers, retail personnel, parking attendants, landscapers, and housekeepers – not to mention complete staffs for the winery and hotel on the huge estate.

"This is so cool," Jack proclaimed, as they looked for their car after a full day of trying to see as much of the Biltmore as humanly possible. A shuttle had picked them up back at the mansion and deposited them at one of the many parking lots on the estate – hopefully the right one, where their car would be patiently waiting.

"Would you want to work here, Jack? Everyone we encountered was very friendly and helpful."

"That's what they pay them to be, I guess. The winery was pretty interesting. I wouldn't want to be on the production end, but maybe dealing with the visitors somehow. You know how I like to talk to people…."

"Yes, I do. Maybe in the wine shop, although you don't drink it yourself."

"I could still learn about wine, to answer questions."

"I can see it all now – someone asks you for a recommendation, and you have to admit that you've never tasted any of their wines. They probably wouldn't hire you in the tasting room…."

"I wouldn't want to be a sommelier, anyway. But did you see the people working in the winery welcome center? Their job just seemed to be talking to those who were waiting in line for a tour of the winemaking process. I think I could handle that."

"No doubt. You could tell them funny stories, and make them forget how long they'd been waiting."

———

Jack applied to the Biltmore and was hired part-time, although he was really needed in the winery's retail shop. His job was to rove the aisles, offering assistance and answering questions, so he was happy to be using his gift of gab – and being paid to do it! Later, he requested a transfer to the welcome center, where he kept young families occupied in line by providing small bags of pretzels from the shop's inventory to their restless children. He didn't ask permission – he just did it – and everyone was glad he did. When Amelia came by to shop for wine, with his employee's discount, he arranged for the sommelier to offer her a free glass of their sparkling wine in the tasting area.

Now it was Amelia's turn to find a job. She hadn't taught for the last twenty years, while she was working for the federal government in Maryland.

This time around she'd try for college-level students, though, and she sent her résumé to six colleges and universities in the area. She got various responses, ranging from "no current openings" to one from a small private college that asked her to "submit a two-page letter outlining your Christian beliefs." Placing all those replies in the trash pile, the only promising one was from the westernmost campus of the University of North Carolina. But it was fifty miles away from where she lived!

The acting head of the Modern Foreign Language Department invited her for an interview, and hired her on the spot to teach French part-time. It seemed that their French professor was retiring, and she could begin in September. That only gave her a matter of weeks to prepare, but Amelia said yes. She had always been the carpe-diem kid, after all, and rarely turned down any opportunity. She found out that she would have to share an office with another new instructor, however, since the foreign language building was being renovated. No problem. She would only be on campus three days a week.

When Amelia met her new office mate, the woman was introduced to her as Sister Evelyn. Hmm…. She was also around sixty years old and had just been hired to teach Spanish. They formed an immediate bond. "I live near the campus, Amelia. How about you?"

"Unfortunately, my husband and I already bought a new house in West Asheville, so it'll be one hundred miles round trip, Sister."

"Oh, please – call me Evelyn! That's the name they gave me when I entered the convent as a young woman. Are you a Catholic, by any chance?"

"As a matter of fact, I was raised a Catholic but I haven't gone to church regularly for a long time. It's complicated.   Maybe I'll tell you about it sometime…."

"Of course. I'm a good listener, Amelia. If you have some time right now, sit down and let's compare our teaching schedules. It looks like we'll have to share this desk and office until they're done renovating."

"I don't mind. I'm only teaching M-W-F mornings, and it's too far for me to drive back and forth any other days!"

2

Sister Evelyn told Amelia that she was sharing a duplex near the campus with another nun from her order, the School Sisters of Notre Dame. They had only allowed Evelyn to accept the teaching position at Western Carolina University (WCU) because she would be living near Sister Agnes, who was already teaching there herself. The idea of living "in community" with other members of their order was a top priority. Agnes taught mathematics, and it didn't seem to matter that they hardly ever saw each other, except on weekends. Even then, Evelyn sometimes ended up spending the weekend with Amelia and Jack, just to have a break from school.

"I love your house here in West Asheville, Amelia. It has the feel of a country setting, with lots of open land and wooded areas. All you need now is a dog, to complete your little family."

"*What?* We're done raising our kids! Why would we want to go back into the business of house-breaking a puppy? Especially now that we're both working part-time."

"But you said yourself that you and Jack have different work schedules. A dog would keep each of you company when you're here alone."

"See…?" Jack came in from puttering around in the garage. "Evelyn is on *my* side!"

"I didn't know we were choosing *sides*. I like dogs as much as you do, Jack!"

"Let's call a truce," Evelyn laughed. "You could always find a dog that needs a good home – one that's already housebroken."

"Maybe, but we're still getting settled," Amelia protested. Give *us* a break…."

"Okay, but I'm not giving up. I need my dog fix when I visit you, since our landlord won't let us have one…where Agnes and I live."

—

Amelia thought that was the end of it for a while, until Jack's twelve-year-old granddaughter Jen arrived from Florida for a short visit. Her family had several cats and dogs! After a few days, Jen handed down her proclamation, as only a twelve-year-old can.

"Papa, I hate to tell you this, but your house is boring. You need a dog."

What can you say to *that*? "I'm sorry you feel that way, Jen," Jack replied, "but we're still unpacking boxes here. How about we all go to a movie this afternoon? You can pick one…."

That seemed to appeal to her, and soon they were on the road to the Biltmore Square Mall – everything was named after the Biltmore here – and planning to stop for lunch before the movie. "Wait, pull over here, Papa! At that big pet store! The sign says 'Pet Adoption Day!' Aw…all the dogs and cats are in their crates. Can we just look at them…please?"

"We can look, but not take one home. Agreed?"

"Okay, Papa. This is even better than the movie…."

"Well, at least you won't tell your mother you were bored here. Let's take a look." When they got out of the car, all three went in different directions in the parking lot, up and down the rows of dozens of metal crates. The cats were in a separate area, but they all concentrated on the dogs as if by unspoken agreement. Each crate had a sign that told the dog's name, breed, and age – and gave explicit instructions not to remove the dog from its crate without checking with the adoption personnel.

Amelia had promised herself not to look at the dogs too closely, but one older puppy's soulful brown eyes gazed into hers as she was passing. She stopped, and went over – precipitating an excited round of tail-wagging. Her name was Autumn, she was four months old, and she was a golden retriever/cocker spaniel mix. She looked like a retriever, with silky golden fur, but she had a smaller spaniel head and ears. She was unique, and she knew it. Amelia's family had had a cocker spaniel when she was little, and so had her boys. It was all she could do to tear herself away.

She walked over to where Jen was talking to some kind of a hound dog in his crate. "Your mother would never forgive us if *you* came home with another dog, Jen," she smiled, and her granddaughter nodded.

Meanwhile, Jack was strolling up and down the rows of crates, and he also stopped to return Autumn's gaze. "You're a pretty girl," he smiled at her, and she swished her feathery tail. She reminded him of the golden retrievers his parents always had as he was growing up, and he reached through the bars to pet her. She was eager for any attention, and licked his hand. Jack called to Amelia across the lot, "Did you see this golden, honey? She's very sweet."

"Autumn? Yes…." Amelia and Jen joined him, and now Autumn got very excited and jumped up to greet them. "I agree it's too soon for us here, but she does seem to like us, Jack."

"You should at least think about it, Papa," Jen coaxed…. "I have an idea. Let's go have lunch, like we planned, and you can bounce your objections off of me. It'll help to talk about it. Okay?"

"All right, Jen." Jack put his arm around her. "I'm hungry, anyway. But don't get your hopes up."

They drove to the nearby Apollo Flame, a family Greek/Italian restaurant, and were seated in a booth. "You two sit opposite me," Jen commanded and they complied, knowing they were in for it. "Now, after we order, you bring up all your objections to adopting Autumn – one by one…"

"And you'll shoot them down," Jack laughed. "Okay, number one – we just moved into a new house, and that's demanding all our extra time and energy, just to get settled. Not to mention starting new part-time jobs."

"Okay, first of all, she'd be so happy to live with you, that she'd be grateful for any attention you gave her at all. Besides, you already said that one of you would probably be at home most of the time, when the other one was working."

"That might be true," Amelia joined the conversation, "but we don't really want to take on the job of housebreaking a puppy."

"At four months old, she's probably already housebroken...." Jen shrugged her shoulders. "What else?"

"Well, we'd still have to walk her multiple times a day. We don't have a fenced-in yard, as you know, and Buncombe County has a leash law."

"Which I doubt very much that they enforce, especially out in the countryside where you live. You could let her out to do her business, and I bet she'd come right back and hang out on your front deck. She'd have a bird's-eye view of the whole neighborhood from there, and you could close the gate on the deck to keep her in."

"What do you think, Jack? Are you ready to be a parent again – of a four-legged ball of fur?"

"I don't know – it's a big responsibility...."

"Why don't you try it?" Jen could feel the tide turning in her favor. "If it doesn't work out, I'm sure you could return her to the pet-adoption people. It's not like adopting a child. Besides, I think you already love her...."

"She *does* remind me of the goldens I had as a boy growing up." Jack had a nostalgic look in his eyes.

"Me, too!" Amelia said. "Her face has that playful cocker expression I loved. My boys would be delighted when they visit."

Jen could already taste victory. "Let's go back after lunch, and see her again. Maybe they'll let us take her out of the cage for a little walk. You won't regret it, Papa."

"Have you ever thought about becoming a lawyer?" Amelia asked her.

—

They drove back to the pet-adoption lot after lunch, and there were many more people checking out the dogs and cats than before. Autumn's cage was the last one in that row, and the door was standing open. She was gone…. "Oh, no! We were only away for an hour!" Jen was beside herself. "How could she have been adopted so quickly?"

"Let's check with the organizers," Jack said, and they walked over to the table with all the necessary paperwork stacked up. "We wanted to see Autumn again," he explained to the woman seated there. "Has she been adopted already?"

"Oh, no. Her foster family had to take her home for the day. They'll be back tomorrow morning, I think."

Amelia jumped in. "It's just that we were thinking of adopting her ourselves." She couldn't hide her disappointment – none of them could.

"Oh, I'm so glad to hear that! Autumn is a very calm, sweet puppy.

16

"She needs a quiet environment to thrive, I think. She was already adopted once, but had to be returned because the family became overwhelmed with caring for their elderly parents. So she's back with her foster family, that has a house full of kids and pets. Do you have other pets, Mr.....?"

"Flynn – Amelia and Jack Flynn. No, it's just the two of us. My granddaughter is visiting, and we've recently moved here from Maryland."

"Judging from your ages, Mr. and Mrs. Flynn, I think that Autumn would be very happy living in a settled household like yours. I'll give you her foster family's phone number, and you can take it from there. If you decide to adopt Autumn, you can contact me about the paperwork. Here's my card. There is a nominal adoption fee, to cover her shots and spaying. I hope it works out for you, and for her. We've become quite attached to her."

Autumn's foster family was thrilled about the prospect of meeting with them several days later, and the Flynns ended up taking her home with them. Unfortunately, Jen had already left to fly back to Florida, but she couldn't wait to come back again with her family, to see Autumn. She had pulled off quite a coup, and everyone was happy. They outfitted Autumn with all the accouterments of her new lifestyle, and showered her with love. She took to her fourth home with gusto, and very soon Amelia and Jack couldn't imagine their life without her.

Her foster family had told them the sad story of Autumn's early life. Her father was a golden retriever in the neighborhood, and her mother was a cocker spaniel. When she had her litter, the owner of the spaniel neglected her, and she was forced to hide the puppies under the front porch. When the mother spaniel was gone to search for food for herself, a hawk swooped down to steal some of the puppies and neighbors reported the owner to the SPCA (Society for the Prevention of Cruelty to Animals). They came and rescued the mother and her remaining litter, including Autumn.

When the puppies were weaned, they and their mother were placed in foster families until they were adopted. Autumn was given her name, but then shuttled back and forth until she finally found her forever home with Amelia and Jack. Even though Jen was directly responsible for getting the ball rolling, Autumn's adoptive parents always felt that fate had also played a part. They were meant to take her into their home, and she was always destined to be their one and only grand-dog.

3

By Christmas, Amelia and Jack had bumped into Phil numerous times at the grocery store and around West Asheville, but they never had time to talk. Then Amelia saw him in the congregation as she sang Christmas Eve Mass with the St. Eugene choir. He happened to be sitting next to Jack, and she met up with them after Mass. "Merry Christmas, Phil!" She hugged him. "This is the first time I've seen you here, since…"

"Since my mother's funeral…I know. I always came with her on Christmas Eve, so here I am. You two must feel like natives by now. How's it going?"

"Slowly, but surely," Jack laughed. "We still haven't mastered the difference between *y'all* and *all y'all*."

"It's tricky. Basically it's singular vs. plural. You might ask me, 'How are y'all doing?' and I'd reply, 'Fair to middling. How are all y'all?'"

"I think I'll stick to 'How are you and Lorraine doing, Phil?'"

"We actually broke up after my mother's funeral, but we're still friends – long-distance friends, since she's in Wilmington, North Carolina. She decided that's where she belongs, and I belong here, so…."

"I'm sorry to hear that," Amelia sympathized. "Anyone new on the horizon?"

"Well, I've been dating a woman named Nora. She was my mother's day-nurse at home until she died. We just sort of gravitated together after that, I guess. She's got a heart of gold."

"I'm glad, Phil. Everyone needs someone special in their lives. Jack and I have been talking about driving over to see the Outer Banks, maybe in March when WCU is on spring break. Could we call Lorraine when we're in Wilmington? I'm not sure she'd remember us from the day of your mother's funeral, when we met her at your house afterwards."

"I'm sure she would. Here's her phone number – tell her I gave it to you. I bet she will at least meet you for dinner.

"Let her know I think of her often, and hope she's doing well."

"That sounds like something *you* should tell her yourself, Phil, but I'll let her know we saw you. Thanks."

———

Lorraine was very gracious on the phone, when Amelia called her. "Of course I remember you and Jack. It was a difficult day for all of us, but I'm glad you took the time to join us. I know it meant a lot to Phil."

"Thank you. We see him around town, and he was good enough to give us your number when we said we were going to be sightseeing in your area in mid-March. We'd love to get together when we're in Wilmington, if you have the time."

"That would be fun, Amelia, although it's still pretty chilly here in March. I know a restaurant with a cozy fireplace, though. Text me your dates, and I'll show you around when you're here."

Their drive to the coast was long, Route 40 all the way, since they had decided to start in Wilmington first. After seeing Lorraine, they would continue north along the Outer Banks. She met them at their downtown hotel, and played tour guide as they walked around the 300-year-old port of Wilmington.

When they were ready for drinks and dinner, Lorraine took them to a local seafood restaurant where they could relax and talk. "So, how do you two like West Asheville?" she asked, after they ordered.

"It's like a small town all its own," Amelia replied. "You can find everything you want…"

"Except the Biltmore Estate, or a university campus, or the church you go to," Jack pointed out.

"Yes, but those things are only twenty minutes away, at most, without having to live in the city."

"I understand what you're both saying. I grew up in West Asheville, until I went away to college and grad school, and then moved to Wilmington. My brother Jeff is still there, but I don't think I could ever go back – permanently, I mean."

"Phil told us that you two have decided to just be friends," Jack blurted out, and Amelia rolled her eyes.

"That's really none of our business, Lorraine," she said, "but I'm sorry we won't be seeing you very much there."

"Me, too, Amelia. Maybe if Jeff and Eric ever get married – or if Phil takes the plunge. Do you know if he's seeing anyone now?"

"I'm not sure…maybe you should ask him yourself, as one friend to another." There. She'd planted the seeds in both of their heads, and now it was up to them.

———

"Are you playing matchmaker, Amelia?" Jack asked, as they proceeded to drive up the coast of North Carolina the next day.

"They're both good people, and we don't know anything about Nora the nurse. So, why not?"

"Because it's none of your business, that's why not, and you just told Lorraine that yesterday!"

"Don't pretend you're not curious about Nora, Jack. Maybe we'll get to meet her sometime."

Autumn ran out to meet them when they returned from their road trip, accompanied by her new friend, Sister Evelyn. It had been a mini-vacation for Evelyn, too, and she enjoyed pretending it was her house and her puppy. Of course, Autumn was almost full-grown now, even though she still behaved like a puppy. That was the thing about golden retrievers, her vet told them. They don't settle down until they're three years old or so. Autumn didn't know that, though. She just knew she loved to run and jump and swim and play – and ride in the car with her head out the window.

Evelyn was a social being, who didn't really like living alone. She had been the oldest of many children in her mid-western family, and had entered the convent as a teenager. In those days, she wore the habit of her religious order, although now she was allowed to dress like everyone else. The small cross around her neck was the only thing that singled her out. "Autumn and I had a great time together, Amelia. It'll be hard going back to classes next week, but I'll be glad to dog-sit anytime you need me."

"Thanks, but we'll have to save up our pennies before we can afford to take another trip, Evelyn. Is it true that we can move into our permanent offices when we go back to school?"

"That's the word. Supposedly they're finishing up the renovations in our building over spring break. We'll find out next week, I guess."

"You're lucky that you were hired full-time, Evelyn. You get a bigger office, with a window!"

"And lots more classes to teach! But I thought you *wanted* to be part-time, Amelia."

"I do, and so does Jack, at the Biltmore. It's a trade-off, just like everything else in life."

"What did you gain when you stopped going to church regularly, as you told me you did, Amelia?"

"Is this a trick question?" she laughed.

"It wasn't *meant* to be. I was just wondering. You said you'd tell me sometime...."

I guess I stopped going because I was mad at God, or maybe disappointed in Him. He let my previous husband walk out on me and my kids, so I stopped visiting Him at church. Unfortunately, I didn't gain *anything*, much less peace of mind. I was more alone than ever, until I met Jack and we got married and then moved here to North Carolina fifteen years later. Then I decided to try again here, and we joined St. Eugene Church. It feels good to be back, and I sing with the choir, too. That's how I met Phil Clark and his friends. I told you about them...."

"Yes. Would it be all right if I joined you some Sunday for Mass?"

"Anytime! You could sing with us in the choir! Do you like to sing, Evelyn?"

"Haven't you ever heard of the Singing Nun? That could have been me, becoming famous by making records like she did! I love to sing! In fact, some weekend, bring an overnight bag and stay with *me*. I'll take you to my Saturday night Mass for the WCU Catholic students on campus. You can sing with me, to lead them in the hymns.

———

Amelia took Evelyn up on it, and Jack didn't mind being on his own for the weekend.

Every Saturday night while school was in session, the students converted a meeting room in the Student Center into a chapel of sorts. They rearranged the chairs, used a table for the altar, and the Catholic university chaplain celebrated the Mass. That's when Amelia found out that Sister Evelyn could play the guitar – and very well! She brought her own guitar, and began to play as the students filtered in. There must have been thirty or so, by the time the Mass started.

"Do you know 'Gather Us In'?" Evelyn asked. Amelia nodded, and they started singing. She looked over Evelyn's shoulder at the words on her sheet music, but the students all seemed to know them by heart. Their enthusiasm was contagious and Amelia wished that her church choir had that many members! Some of the girls wore mantillas, folded their hands prayerfully as they came up to receive the Eucharist, and the chaplain celebrated the Mass in Latin for them! It felt very retro, but then college students always did rebel against current norms.

Amelia recognized one of her French students in the group, and remembered how the girl had come to her after class one day. Amelia had been showing the class an R-rated movie in French, and the girl had asked if she were required to watch the rest of it during the next class later that week. Amelia excused her without penalty, but found it unusual that a nineteen-year-old would object to an R-rated movie in this day and age. It was basically a comedy, but did contain some student bed-hopping.

After Amelia thought about it, however, she realized that the reason her students were such a pleasure to teach was that most of them were the first generation of college students in their families. They came from farming communities in the mountains of Western North Carolina, and were invariably polite. Their parents had sacrificed to send them to college, and expected them to remain in the area when they graduated. That wasn't always what their offspring wanted, however.

One of her hardest-working students was a boy who had dreams of becoming a French-trained chef, and he wanted to learn French in order to attend the *Cordon Bleu* cooking school in Paris as part of a WCU junior-year-abroad program. His parents forbade him to travel to France, however, and he ended up transferring to a local community college near Asheville to study cuisine. It broke Amelia's heart, but the boy was resigned to abiding by his parents' wishes. That was simply the way he was raised.

Amelia had a lot to learn from her students and also her new friends – much more than she could ever hope to teach *them*!

4

Although they didn't know it at the time, Amelia and Jack were about to meet the current woman in Phil's life – since they had already met Derek's mother Alicia, and Phil's other former girlfriend Lorraine. Phil had certainly led a complicated life, where women were concerned. And all three still seemed to be interested in him, or at least concerned about him. It happened at the grocery store, of all places – in the fresh produce area. Phil noticed them perusing the heads of lettuce, and came over. "Amelia…Jack! We have to stop meeting like this," Phil laughed.

They looked up, each one holding their own chosen head of lettuce. "Hi, Phil!" Amelia smiled, tossing hers in the cart.

"This is my girlfriend, Nora," he said, a touch of pride in his voice.

"It's nice to meet you, Nora." Amelia extended her hand. "We don't live that far from Phil, so we see him occasionally here. We just moved to North Carolina last summer…."

"Then we must get together sometime," Nora suggested, and Phil nodded. The two couples parted ways, leaving it at that.

"She's a lot younger than Lorraine or Alicia," Amelia commented to Jack when they were out of earshot. "But she seems nice."

"All that matters is what Phil thinks," Jack decided, and Amelia couldn't argue with that….

"Why don't we invite them over for dinner some weekend, when I'm at your house, Phil?" Nora proposed. "It's really hard to make friends when you're new to the area."

"They might think they're too old to hang out with us, Nora, but Amelia was very kind to me when my mother died."

"All the more reason to invite them, then."

———

It took some finagling to arrange a get-together at Phil's house, but Amelia and Jack finally arrived at his door one Saturday evening, a bottle of Biltmore wine in hand.

"I hope you like the estate wine," Jack said, handing it to Phil. "I'm working at their winery part-time now."

"You might say I was raised on it! Thanks, Jack. Do they keep you busy stomping on the grapes?"

"Not yet, thankfully. I'm working in the welcome center right now."

"Let's go out in the kitchen and open it. Nora's busy whipping up something special for us. She's a great cook."

"Hi, Nora! Can we help – or at least pour you a glass of wine?" Amelia asked. "It smells wonderful in here!"

"I'm just keeping an eye on the *boeuf bourguignon* at the moment, but I'd love a glass of wine, Amelia."

"Make mine a soda, Phil, or anything else non-alcoholic," Jack said.

"A teetotaler working in a winery? Now I've heard everything, Jack!"

"I was hired for my gift of gab, and my good looks," Jack laughed.

"Well, that explains it…. Turn down the burner and let's all sit down together, Nora. I'll come out and stir it whenever you say so."

"Okay…. So, are you working part-time, too, Amelia?"

"Yes, I've gone back to teaching French, but this time at the college level – at WCU."

"You drive all the way out there? I hope they pay you well." Phil just shook his head.

"They don't, since I'm adjunct faculty, but I also don't have the extra responsibilities that full-time instructors have, like student advisees and more classes. I just drive in, teach my two classes, and leave. It's great."

"We even adopted a puppy from the local rescue organization – a golden retriever mix, named Autumn. She's our grand-dog." Jack proudly showed them her picture on his phone.

"What a sweetie-pie! Bring her over sometime," Nora said. "But call first, to make sure Phil's home."

"Where do you work, Phil?" Amelia asked.

"I'm one of the managers of a medium-sized hotel in Asheville. Now that I moved back to West Asheville, I drive in every day, but not as far as *you* do, Amelia!"

"Luckily, I only have to be on campus three mornings a week, so it's not that bad. How about you, Nora?"

"Well, I'm a nurse at Mission Hospital in Asheville. I live near here, but Phil and I have different schedules, so we can't really drive in together. It's complicated…."

Amelia wondered why they weren't living together like most young couples did, but of course she didn't ask. When Nora got up to go and check on the beef stew, Amelia decided to mention something else that was on her mind. "We had dinner with Lorraine when we were in Wilmington, Phil. She showed us all around town, too. It was great."

"I'm glad you saw her, and I'm not surprised that she went out of her way to entertain you. That's just the kind of person she is – always thinking of others." It sounded like Phil wished she would think about *him* sometimes, too….

—

"Who *are* these new friends of our son's, Alice?" Daniel had died years ago, but his wife Alice's spirit had only joined him six months ago.

"Don't you remember, Daniel? Amelia sang at my funeral, and offered Phil her condolences. She and her husband Jack were new in town, and Phil has befriended them.

"They live nearby, and Nora thought it would be nice to invite them over for dinner."

"Nora was your day-nurse after your first stroke, right? She seems to have picked right up with Phil where Lorraine left off! Young women today don't miss a beat, do they?"

"Well, Phil is a bit shy with women, so they have to take the lead. It's a shame that Lorraine gave up on him, though. We've known her all her life – living right next door, with her big brother, Jeff."

"And now Jeff is living there with his boyfriend, Eric. It's a topsy-turvy world, isn't it, Alice?"

"Yes, but at least everyone back home is happy, for now. I'm not sure about Lorraine, though, all the way over in Wilmington…."

Lorraine's late parents, Jane and Robert, had to comment on that. "I worry about her," Jane's spirit said. "She works too hard."

"At least she's not in one of those same-sex relationships, like her brother!" Robert's spirit had always been very clear about his feelings in that regard.

"Do you think that Derek's mother, Alicia, has changed her mind about Phil?" Alice inquired, of no one in particular.

"I did hear her having a heart-to-heart talk with him after you died, Alice," Jane said. "It sounded like Alicia was ready to settle down then – with Phil. Too bad she didn't figure that out sooner. If you snooze, you lose."

"It would certainly be a good thing for Derek if his parents got back together," Daniel said, "but that's not looking too good at the moment, I'm afraid."

—

Alicia was also an experienced nurse, who worked at the Haywood Regional Hospital, half an hour west of Asheville. It would have been awkward if she and Nora were working at the same hospital, Phil thought. Alicia had custody of their thirteen-year-old son, Derek, who spent at least one weekend a month with Phil. Nora didn't want to infringe on his precious time with his son, so she usually made her own plans on those weekends. The two women had met each other, of course, but tried to stay out of one another's way.

"Are you dropping me off at Daddy's house this weekend, Momma?" Derek asked, when he got home from school.

"Yes. We talked about it this week, remember? Is that still okay with you?"

"Sure. We go to movies you probably wouldn't like, and play video games. Then we get a pizza when we're hungry, and it doesn't even matter what time of day it is. It's pretty cool."

"It sounds like it. Derek, would you ever want me to come out for pizza with you guys…or to a movie? I mean, if it's something I'd like to see, too."

"It's okay with me, but you'd better ask him. He usually has plans for when I come over."

"Okay, well, get your stuff and let's go. It's getting late, and the traffic will be heavy…."

Alicia usually just dropped Derek off in front of Phil's house, but this time she came in with him. "Hey, Daddy, we're here," Derek called out when they walked in, and Phil came downstairs.

"Hey, buddy…hi, Alicia. How *are* you? Is anything wrong?"

"No, not at all, Phil. I just wanted to talk to you for a minute."

"Sure. Why don't you take your stuff upstairs, Derek, and see what's on TV for a few minutes."

"Okay. See you, Momma…."

"Come in and sit down, Alicia. How have you been?"

"Honestly…? I've been missing you, Phil. I know that sounds weird, after thirteen years, but I guess raising Derek alone is harder now that he's a teenager."

"I'm sure that's true. He could spend more time with *me* here, if that would help."

"He'd love that, but *I'd* like to spend some time with you, too, Phil…. Could I cook you both dinner, or maybe go out for pizza with you?"

Phil knew what was on her mind, and he wasn't sure what to say. "I don't think that's a good idea, Alicia…. What purpose would it serve? You wanted your own life, with Derek, and now you have it. I've made a life for myself, too, and Nora is part of that life now. She gives me space when Derek is here, but eventually I want to form a family together with her, and Derek. She's my future, Alicia, and you're my past. I was hoping that you would move on with *your* life, too."

"I tried, but nothing compares to what we had together, Phil."

"We were young, and had stars in our eyes. Reality is more complicated than we ever realized then, Alicia, and we can't go back to those days – I don't even want to. I wish you all the best that life has to offer, but I can't share it with you. I'm sorry…."

Alicia knew she had lost him for good, but she was too tired to fight it anymore. "Tell Derek I'll pick him up on Sunday afternoon, as usual." She got up and gave Phil a hug, before walking out the door. He didn't feel relief, or even guilt…just a heavy sadness.

5

When Amelia felt the need to start getting some regular exercise, as she had done in Maryland, she tried out a group class at Haywood Regional Health and Fitness Center. It was adjacent to the hospital where Derek's mother Alicia worked, but that was neither here nor there. Amelia had a hard time approaching new situations on her own, but she was determined to give it a try one Tuesday morning. The class was held on Tuesdays and Thursdays, which meshed with her M-W-F teaching schedule, so she took the stairs to the second floor, where she was told the class would take place.

She almost collided with runners at the top of the staircase, who were using the indoor track! Since she was early and she saw some walkers on the track, too, she decided to see where it led and began to walk in the same direction.

Overhead signs cautioned walkers to stay to the right, so that runners could pass them, and another sign informed everyone that the traffic direction on the track changed every day from right to left at the top of the stairs. Very well organized, she thought, as she walked along.

Amelia passed a middle-aged woman who looked as though she were auditioning for a Broadway musical – dancing down the track and reaching her arms this way and that. It was comical, although the woman was taking it very seriously. Someone at the front desk had told Amelia that three laps would equal one mile, but she didn't have time for that today. When she reached the turn in the track, however, she saw that the whole side wall suddenly became a floor-to-ceiling window, and the view of the Blue Ridge Mountains in the distance was stupendous! Worth the cost of the membership itself!

After one lap, she braved the door to the group-exercise room and was glad she wasn't the first to arrive. A few women of various ages had deposited their gym bags along the back wall, and were heading to the adjoining equipment room. Amelia did the same, and saw row upon row of large inflated balls for the taking. She chose a big one, being tall herself, and smiled at the others. She was happy she had brought her exercise mat, too, which everyone else seemed to be using to reserve their spot in the room, bouncing on their balls while they waited for the instructor to show up.

The room had a full-length mirror on the side everyone was facing, like a ballet studio, which was a bit intimidating. The opposite wall was all window, looking back out at the track. There appeared to be about fifteen women in the class, talking and waiting. The door opened, and an older woman came in – obviously not the instructor, since she scurried to her usual spot behind Amelia, dropped her belongings, and went in search of a ball. When she rolled her ball out and sat down on it, she called out, "Are you new? Welcome!"

Since she could only be addressing *her*, Amelia turned around, self-conscious at being singled out. "Hi," the woman said with a smile. "I'm Annie."

"I'm Amelia, and I *am* new here. Hi, Annie."

"Here comes the instructor." Annie looked over at the door. "Maybe we can talk afterward, if you have time."

"Sure. If I'm still among the living…."

Their instructor was probably in her fifties, which surprised Amelia, but it meant that the woman was very aware of the challenges faced by students of a certain age. Amelia felt comfortable with the routine, and was looking forward to talking to Annie after the hour-long class.

"Let's walk the track while we talk," Annie suggested, and Amelia agreed. "So, are you new to the *area*, too?"

"The area, the state – you name it! My husband and I moved here from Maryland last autumn, thinking of early retirement. That didn't work out financially, so we both went back to work – I'm teaching French at WCU, and he works at the Biltmore Estate winery's welcome center."

"I'm surprised you even have *time* for an exercise class, but I'm glad you do! I live near here, at Lake Junaluska, and I'm most definitely retired – but I'm probably at least ten years older than you, Amelia."

"I find that hard to believe, Annie, but I'll take your word for it."

"You'll have to, because a lady never tells her age…. If you come to class on Thursday, how about walking halfway around the lake with me afterwards? There's a great little coffee-and-gift shop along the way – my treat."

"It's a date, if the weather cooperates. Thanks, Annie."

—

Amelia was excited to spend time with Annie, who made her want to go back to the exercise class again just to see her.

Friendship and exercise, all rolled into one! It seemed like new friends were appearing in her life when, and where, she needed them the most. Was it coincidence, or was some other unseen force at work in her new life here in North Carolina? Whatever it was, she wouldn't question it – just enjoy it. She couldn't wait for Thursday to roll around.

Annie was in class, and they left together. "Follow me over to my condo, Amelia, and park in one of the unnumbered spaces. The lake is right beside my complex." She wasn't kidding. As soon as they parked, they were walking on the path that led around Lake Junaluska. Halfway around, a little foot bridge crossed to the other side, and they came to a community center where the coffee shop was. Amelia wanted to look at the handmade gifts first, before settling down with coffee on the patio that overlooked the lake.

It was a peaceful spot, and a family of swans swam slowly by. "You must love it here, Annie."

"I do, and my daughter and her little family live nearby. I moved here from mid-state some years ago, when my husband died."

"I'm sorry to hear that, Annie."

"Don't be. It wasn't a happy marriage, and I'm much more content with my life here. I have my church, and my granddaughter nearby, too."

"What church do you go to?"

"A Catholic church in the area. The only objection I have is that the Jesuit pastor is always pleading with the congregation to donate more money. It gets tiresome after a while...."

"I go to a Catholic church, too, in Asheville. You should come with me sometime, Annie. I sing in the choir, but after Mass some of us go out to lunch together. I'd love it if you joined us sometime. The atmosphere in my parish isn't anything like yours. Our pastor is only in his thirties, and he's very laid-back. We call him our 'baby priest.' Will you come sometime soon? It wouldn't take you more than half an hour to drive in."

"Well, if you can drive over *here* twice a week, I guess I have no excuse. How long does it take you to drive to the WCU campus where you teach?"

"An hour each way, but only three times a week."

"It's a good thing you're young, Amelia. It makes me tired just thinking about your schedule!"

—

Annie met Amelia at her church in Asheville the very next Sunday, and it warmed Amelia's heart to look out from the choir and see her sitting in the congregation.

She leaned over to the soprano next to her, her new friend Trish, and pointed Annie out to her before the Mass started. "I asked her to join our lunch bunch today. Is that okay with you, Trish?"

"Everyone will be delighted to meet a friend of yours, Amelia. Where should we go?"

"How about trying that new restaurant just up the road from here? It's gotten good reviews."

"Sounds like a plan."

Annie fit right in with the lunch bunch, mainly because she was so easygoing. Too bad she didn't sing! Before long she left her local church behind, and began coming to St. Eugene Church regularly.

"Who the heck was St. Eugene, anyway?" Annie wondered.

"He was our pope around 600 A.D., I think," Amelia offered, between sips of her mimosa. They limited themselves to one drink each, since they were all driving. It did her heart good to watch Annie and Trish, two of her special new friends, interacting so easily. They had a lot in common, but never would have met without Amelia's invitation. Life was funny that way. One thing led to another, and suddenly Amelia was starting to fit into her new surroundings after all.

—

Amelia still hadn't found a movie buddy in Asheville, though – someone to go with her to chick-flicks that Jack refused to go and see. She made her pitch to Sr. Evelyn one weekend when her friend was visiting overnight with them. "Come to see a movie with me, Evelyn! I'm dying to check out the remake of 'Anna Karenina,' and Jack has absolutely no interest in going."

"Okay, and then I'll come to church with you tomorrow before I leave. I've got a ton of papers to correct when I get home. What's the movie about?"

"Oh, the usual period piece. A married woman falls in love with a handsome officer, and it doesn't end well. It's an R-rated movie, though – probably for the sex, I'm guessing. Is that all right with you?"

"As long as it's not X-rated, I think I can handle it, Amelia. I come from a big family, remember?"

The movie was amazing, and totally did justice to Leo Tolstoy's novel, but Evelyn had a serious expression on her face as they walked out of the theater. "Too much hanky-panky, Evelyn?"

"No…it's just that the ending was so sad! Realistic, but sad. Don't we have enough sadness in this world?"

"*C'est la vie!* Unless you live in Newfoundland….

"I've heard it said that when they die and go to heaven, they just want to go home!"

"How would anyone even know that, Amelia?"

"It's a joke, Evelyn…."

"Not a very good one, though."

Amelia was excited for Evelyn to sing in the choir with her on Sunday. Her choir director gave her the okay, since Evelyn probably already knew all the hymns and Mass parts they had rehearsed. Annie was in the congregation, as usual; Evelyn and Trish were on either side of Amelia; and she was thankful to have her new friends all together that day. Moving to North Carolina had been a leap of faith, but it had brought Amelia back to her roots in many ways.

Now she'd have to work on Trish and Annie to go to chick-flicks with her on the Sundays when Evelyn wasn't around! But first the three musketeers welcomed Evelyn into their lunch bunch, and let her choose the restaurant. She chose a Mexican place, where she could use her Spanish with the employees, and everyone else just enjoyed their tacos and such – not to mention the pitcher of sangria!

6

There were lots of changes taking place that spring, in Amelia's life and in the lives of her new friends. Renovations of the language building on campus were complete, and Amelia was excited to move into her own office. Sharing an office with Evelyn was fun at first, but they had to stagger their use of its only desk and Evelyn really needed it every day. Being part-time had its disadvantages, and that was certainly one of them for Amelia. If they hadn't been friends, it would have been impossible, but Evelyn tried her best to absent herself on the three mornings a week that Amelia was there.

Finally, the department secretary presented Amelia with her very own office key, and she walked down the hall to take a look. The sign on the door read, "Room 131A, Amelia Flynn, French Instructor," and she turned the key in the lock.

She had been told that it would be small, but she wasn't prepared for a windowless room the size of a pantry. There was barely enough space for the desk, two chairs (one for her and one for a visiting student), a small bookcase, and a trash can. She draped her jacket over the extra chair, and left the door open for ventilation and to combat claustrophobia. Then she got busy hanging posters of France, and turning on her CD player to let French folksongs wash over her as she sat down and closed her eyes. A knock on her open door brought her back to her senses. There stood the acting department head who had hired her, whose office opened off the same little alcove as hers. She could see by glancing through *his* open office door that he had much more space, not to mention numerous windows that provided a view of the campus. It went with the territory, she supposed.

"Getting settled?" he smiled.

"Not much room for clutter – I guess that's a good thing."

"You've had great evaluations so far, Amelia. I hope you'll stay with us for as long as you can."

"That's the plan. Thanks. As long as I can still afford gas for the car, I'll be around."

"Good…."

—

Amelia decided to walk down the hall and see if Evelyn was in her new office yet. She could hear the sound of castanets, likely accompanying Spanish music, before she even got to her office door. Great minds think alike…. But Evelyn wasn't sitting, she was filling up her bookshelf. "Hey, this is nice!" Amelia said, as she walked in. Evelyn had windows, too, and a bigger desk than Amelia's. Oddly enough, there wasn't any jealousy involved, though. Amelia had a husband and a home, and a puppy. But this job was really all Evelyn had that belonged to her.

By the time June rolled around, the school year was over, and Amelia had heard through the neighborhood grapevine that Nora had moved in with Phil in West Asheville. She remembered that they had started dating after his mother's funeral, about ten months ago. That's about how long Amelia and Jack had already lived in North Carolina, too! How the time had flown by! Phil had even mentioned that his best friend Jeff next door had been living there with his partner Eric for about a year now. So both couples were staying in the Clarks' and Walkers' family homes. Phil's and Jeff's late parents must be so proud of their sons for not moving away!

"Let's invite all four of them for dinner, Jack!" Amelia surprised him with the idea, after telling him about Nora moving in with Phil.

"Only if you make it a pot-luck dinner, Amelia. I don't want you spending all day in the kitchen, cooking for a bunch of kids who are half our age!"

"Oh, all right. In fact, Nora isn't much more than a third of our age, but she's a fantastic cook. Remember her *boeuf bourguignon*?"

"Yes! Maybe she'd make that again, now that she's more familiar with Phil's kitchen."

"Good idea! I'll make dessert…so what should we ask the boys to bring?"

"How about salad and rolls? It's hard to screw that up…."

"Right. I'll let Phil pick a weekend that Derek won't be staying with them. His time with his son comes first."

"And we'll be able to have adult conversations without Derek here," Jack added.

——

Everyone thought that a pot-luck dinner was a great idea, and they all showed up at Amelia and Jack's house with their contributions to the meal proudly in hand.

"Hi, Amelia," Nora greeted her with a smile. "This stew can sit on a low burner, just to keep it hot until we're ready to eat."

"It smells wonderful," Jack said, hungry already. "Come on in, and welcome."

"Your house is really open and spacious," Phil noted. "We've never seen the inside...."

"It's an optical illusion." Jack pointed to the cathedral ceiling in the family room. "The whole house is only 1,700 square feet." Autumn had barked when they came to the door, but now that they were welcomed inside she switched into tail-wagging mode. "How about a glass of wine – Biltmore, of course," he stated proudly.

"That would be super," Nora said, setting down the pot of beef stew on the stove. "It's been a busy Saturday, and I'm ready to relax."

They all accepted a glass of rosé, except Jack, who answered the next knock on the door. "Hey, guys! Welcome to our home!" Jeff and Eric came in, bearing gifts of food to round out the meal.

"This salad can go in the fridge for now," Eric said, "if you have the space. It's a broccoli salad – I hope you like broccoli...."

"Who doesn't like broccoli?" Nora laughed, and nobody dared reply. "What's in your bag, Jeff?"

"I made some biscuits. I hope they're okay."

"That'll go great with the stew, Jeff," Amelia assured him, as she peeked in the bag. Thanks. Have some wine with us."

Jack poured them each a glass, and a soda for himself. "What shall we drink to?"

"Relationships," Nora was quick to answer, holding up her glass and glancing at Phil out of the corner of her eye.

"And marriage." Jeff took Eric's hand, and they both grinned from ear to ear, like Cheshire cats.

"What…?" everyone else blurted out at once!

"I don't believe it!" Phil punched his friend's arm.

"Believe it!" Jeff held up his ring finger, and Eric did the same.

"When did *this* happen?" Phil wouldn't let them off the hook. "We need details!"

"Well, we just looked at each other one morning," Eric said, "and decided to get married. So we went down to the courthouse yesterday, and did the deed. You're not really surprised, are you, Phil?"

Phil was speechless. "Well, *we* are!" Amelia broke the silence. "So, let's raise our glasses to Jeff and Eric – congratulations, and best wishes for a happy future together! I wish this were champagne, but the wine will do nicely for now."

"Don't worry," Jeff said, "we had champagne last night, Amelia, on our wedding night…. And getting together with our friends tonight, old and new, is the best wedding reception we could ever imagine!"

"But you shouldn't have had to help provide the food for it!" Jack was still in disbelief.

"The price was right, Jack. Thanks!" That set the tone for a festive evening, and Jack refilled their glasses. The food was delicious, everyone was in a good mood, and Amelia's chocolate/peanut butter pie was a hit – as a substitute for the wedding cake.

———

Reaction in heaven to this news was mixed. "That's the most ridiculous thing I ever heard of," Jeff's father, Robert, commented to the other three spirits who were gathered around. "I'm not racist or homophobic, but the idea of a black homosexual as my son-in-law is hard for me to wrap my head around. Couldn't they have just continued to live together? That wouldn't have been quite as permanent as getting married…."

"That's the point, Robert," his wife Jane said. "I'm sure that they *want* their relationship to be permanent. Would you have wanted *us* to just live together?"

"That was different, Jane. No couples just lived together back then. It was frowned upon. You either got married or you split up."

"Or you got married, and *then* you split up! Jeff and Eric have lived together for quite a while now. They knew exactly what they were getting into when they got married. I think they have a good chance of make their marriage work." Jane was much less compliant now, where Robert was concerned. *Better late than never*, she reasoned.

"I agree with you," Phil's mother Alice said. "Now that Nora has moved in with Phil, they'll find out all sorts of things about each other. I wish Daniel and I had been able to do that, but I still would have married him eventually, I think."

"I certainly hope so, Sweetheart," Daniel whispered, wishing that spirits could still kiss each other.

—

After the impromptu wedding dinner for Jeff and Eric, the guests all walked the short distance back home together. "I can't get over the fact that you and Eric are married, Jeff," Phil said.

"We can't, either. Who would have thought I'd beat you to the altar, Phil?"

"I never knew it was a competition, or I would have dropped out a long time ago. Now that we're living together, Nora and I are quite happy with the status quo. Right, honey?" Nora just smiled….

"Are you guys planning a honeymoon?" Nora asked.

"Since we don't get paid when we're not teaching, probably not," Eric responded. "Maybe we'll take a stay-cation next week, and just hole up in our house for a while. So if you see lots of grocery and restaurant deliveries, we're probably just hanging out in bed. Don't call *us*, we'll call *you*!"

"Yeah. We'll see you when we see you…. Goodnight, you two." Jeff gave them both a hug.

"Congrats again. You sure know how to keep a secret," Phil smiled, and they parted ways. "I'm still in shock over their announcement, Nora…."

"Lots more exciting than just my moving in with *you*."

"Oh, I don't know about that, honey. My heart still skips a beat when I come home from work and know that you're waiting there for me."

"Unless I'm on a night shift at the hospital, and I'm hoping you haven't already left for Asheville by the time I get home in the morning."

"Probably not the best time to jump into marriage ourselves…."

"Right." But her heart told her otherwise.

7

Amelia's contact with Sr. Evelyn was more sporadic during the summer months, since regular classes weren't in session on campus. Evelyn always traveled to see her family out west then, and only rarely drove in to Asheville to visit Amelia, Jack, and Autumn. Amelia maintained her contact with Annie, however, at regular exercise classes and in church on Sunday. Since the choir had disbanded for the summer, Amelia sat in the congregation with Annie and enjoyed the different perspective it provided on the Mass. Sometimes they were the only members of the lunch bunch present, though.

"Don't you see your kids in the summer, Amelia?" Annie asked, between bites of her smoked-salmon-and-cream-cheese bagel after Mass. It was one of their favorite places to eat when it was just the two of them.

"We'll drive up to Maryland and Pennsylvania before school starts again, and the only other time we see them is over the holidays – if they come down here. Twice a year just isn't enough, though, now that there are grandkids being born. We always miss so much…."

"I'm really lucky to have my daughter and granddaughter near where I live. But that might change at some point, now that I'm getting older…."

"Surely you won't move away from them, the way Jack and I did…."

"Not as far as you did, but I've been looking around at retirement communities in the area, and there's a nice one just south of Asheville, not that far from *you*! It's called Deerfield, and it's an Episcopal community."

"But…"

"Don't worry, you don't have to be Episcopalian to live there. In fact, there are quite a few who aren't – like me."

"That would be pretty cool, Annie! We could see each other more, and go to movies together, and…"

"There's just one downside, Amelia. I wouldn't be in our exercise class anymore.

"It would be too far to drive back there, and exercise classes are included in the cost of this facility, anyway."

"Oh, no! I'd only see you at church on Sunday, or an occasional get-together? That's not enough, Annie!"

"Don't get into a funk, Amelia. I'm just on a waiting list, so who knows when they'll have an opening? When we're done eating you can follow me down there if you have time, and I'll have them give us a tour. Then you'll see how close it is."

Amelia followed Annie's car as she drove due south of Asheville for about twenty minutes, then pulled through the gates and down a winding road that led to the main entrance of Deerfield. They walked into a spacious lounge area, with couches and comfortable chairs arranged in conversational groups. A stone fireplace stood ready for the winter ahead, and residents sat talking together or just wandering through. No one was in a hurry – why *should* they be? Everyone was retired, except the woman behind the welcome desk.

Annie had already told Amelia that her late husband had been a doctor, who left her very comfortable financially when he died. Too bad he hadn't consulted a doctor himself when his health was failing, dying much too young. The woman behind the desk asked if she could help them, and Annie explained who she was.

The receptionist was anxious to please a future resident and her friend, and made a phone call. Within minutes a woman their age appeared, who had volunteered to be on call to show people around. She was a resident, and a very happy one, judging from her demeanor.

"Are you also considering a move here, Mrs. Flynn?" she asked Amelia.

"No, I live in the area, but I was interested in seeing what you have to offer." They were all putting their best foot forward, even though Amelia was already sure that this place would be totally out of her price range. Amelia and Annie had just come from church and were dressed in their Sunday best, so it was fun for Amelia to pretend, just for a little while. As they walked through the facility, she acted as though she and Jack could even consider a place like this if they wanted to.

The woman showed them the library area, the fitness center, a sample apartment, the gift shop, the indoor pool, and finally the dining room. "Would you two like to have dinner with us today – at no cost – just to have an idea of what we offer our residents?"

"That would be nice," Annie replied. "It's buffet, Amelia, so you can just choose what you want." The woman showed them to a table, and then bid them goodbye. They put their purses and jackets down, and a server came over to ask what they'd like to drink.

Then they got in the buffet line with a tray, and chose from entrée items that were plated from behind the steam table. From there, they could choose their own rolls, salad bar items, soup, and a variety of desserts. "If I ate like this every day, I'd blow up like a balloon," Amelia whispered to Annie.

"I'm sure that the novelty wears off, eventually," Annie laughed. "There don't seem to be any obese residents walking around."

"The apartment she showed us was nice, Annie. What size place are you waiting for?"

"One with two bedrooms, and two full baths. That way I could have guests stay overnight – like you, Amelia, or a family member. So, what do you think so far?"

"I think that if I were your age and in your financial position, I would jump at the chance to live here! Put me on your guest list when you get in, Annie!"

It wasn't too long before Deerfield had just the right apartment for Annie – two bedrooms, two baths, a small patio just outside the living room slider, and close access to the parking lot exit. Her family helped her move in, and Amelia was happy for her. She still saw Annie at church on Sundays, but Amelia missed her presence in the exercise class. Now she walked the indoor track alone, and there were no more hikes around Lake Junaluska with a coffee break halfway.

Her friend had gotten her to come to exercise class regularly, but now Amelia had to continue that commitment on her own.

—

Amelia had begun teaching at the Osher Lifelong Learning Institute (OLLI) on the Asheville campus of the University of North Carolina (UNCA) that summer. She was teaching Intermediate French to retired people who wanted to brush up their language skills with an eye to traveling in Europe – or who just regretted not having taken their high school or college French classes seriously enough. She enjoyed teaching dedicated students for a change, which was the only compensation for the otherwise unpaid position. Her students actually begged her for homework – what a concept!

One day, Amelia's student helper, Victoria, who among other things took classroom attendance and checked out the on-loan textbooks for her, invited her to go to the Grove Park Inn's spa complex after class. Amelia's choir friend Trish was in charge of the busy reservation desk there, and it was fun to surprise her. Trish pulled some strings and got the two of them complimentary day passes. Victoria swam in the indoor-to-outdoor pool, while Amelia lounged alongside with a book and a glass of sangria. Massages and the like cost extra, so they saved those for another time. The only thing that would have made the experience more enjoyable was if Trish could have joined them for a while.

Meeting Trish in the first place had been coincidental, if you believe in such things. One Sunday early on, the choir wasn't singing for some reason, so Amelia had sat down in the congregation for Mass. When she noticed that the woman sitting next to her couldn't find a spare hymnal, she shared her own. The first hymn was well-known to both of them and when the woman began to sing, her lovely soprano voice filled the air around them. Amelia just had to get to know her after Mass.

"I'm Amelia Flynn. You have a beautiful voice...."

"Thanks. I'm Trish – pleased to meet you."

"I belong to the choir, and we usually sing this Mass. Have you ever thought about joining the choir? We could really use more sopranos."

"I don't know much about it...."

"Come with me, and I'll introduce you to our choir director, Caroline. She'll answer all your questions, and then some."

Amelia didn't give Trish much of a choice. She took her up to where Caroline had been cantoring during Mass, and introduced her. "I just heard an outstanding soprano voice next to me at Mass, and you might be able to recruit her, Caroline. This is Trish."

"Hi, Trish. Would you like to come to a choir rehearsal, and see if it's something you'd like to do? No pressure…."

"Don't worry, Caroline," Amelia said. "*I* have no qualms about exerting pressure on Trish. I'll threaten her with the rack if I have to," she laughed, but Trish looked worried. "I'm kidding! Let's go get a cup of coffee in the gathering space here, and I'll tell you everything I know about the choir."

"Now *I'm* worried," Caroline smiled. "You two go ahead, and I hope to see you Wednesday night, Trish."

"Thanks. We'll see…."

Amelia and Trish sat together over coffee, as kids ran by with a donut in one hand and a paper cup of lemonade in the other. It was fun to watch, knowing that *they* weren't responsible for them. They shared details about their lives with each other, and when it was time to go they were well on their way to becoming the friends they were meant to be. They both loved to sing, loved their church, and Amelia talked Trish into combining the two by joining the music ministry at St. Eugene.

Trish showed up at the next rehearsal, and they began sitting next to each other in the soprano section from then on – even in the choir on Sundays.

They encouraged each other to come to
rehearsals regularly, even if they had had a hard day
at work. Somehow singing together always put them
in a better frame of mind, and they invariably left
with smiles on their faces.

8

While Jeff and Eric were on their summer vacation from teaching and technically still honeymooners, Jeff decided it was time to announce their marriage to his little sister Lorraine in Wilmington, North Carolina. She had already met Eric at Phil's mother's funeral last summer, and knew that Jeff and Eric were living together next door to him, but their marriage would be news to her – and probably quite a shock! "Why don't you stop talking about it, Jeff, and just pick up the phone and call her?" Eric pleaded.

"I have a better idea, Eric. Let's take the wedding trip we never had, and drive over to Wilmington to tell her in person. She's been trying to get me over there for years, so let's actually do it…but not tell her we're coming!"

"Are you nuts? Your sister is the most organized person I know! She'd hate it if we just drop in, out of the blue! She likes being prepared."

"Well, it's time she got over that. Trust me, she'll be really happy, once she gets over the shock. And when I tell her that we're married, all will be forgiven."

"Okay, I trust you, Jeff. You know Lorraine better than I do. And the idea of our first trip together is too appealing to pass up – just like you are…."

—

Jeff told his friend Phil about their travel plans, and asked him to keep an eye on their house next door. "Sure, Jeff. Give Lorraine a hug for me, and have a great time. You guys deserve it." They decided to leave early in the morning and get to Wilmington the same day, to save money on an overnight. Their GPS dumped them out in front of Lorraine's condo before dark, and Jeff was persuaded to give her a heads-up call rather than just a knock on the door.

"Lorraine? It's Jeff."

"Hey, Jeff. How are things in West Asheville?"

"They were fine when we left this morning, but right now Eric and I are in my car – parked in your condo parking lot…."

Lorraine's tired brain attempted to process this information, and failed. "What's wrong? Has someone died? Phil?"

"No! It's just a surprise visit, Lorraine. You've been nagging me for years to come and see you, so here we are!"

"I can't believe it! Well, come on up – Apt.112." She ran around, picking up stray books, glasses, and throw pillows. Everything came to a halt when they knocked on the door, however. "Come in," she called out, quickly putting the glasses in the sink. "This is a wonderful surprise, big brother," she smiled, hugging both of them. "What's the occasion, or did you just feel guilty for not visiting me sooner?"

"Both, actually." Jeff glanced at Eric, and he nodded. This was Jeff's news to tell his sister, just as Eric had already told his own family. "Eric and I got married in June, and I wanted to tell you in person, Lorraine."

"Oh, Jeff! I'm so happy for both of you!" She gave them a group hug, and they all sat down on the couch together. "Momma and Daddy would be thrilled, and I would have come if you had let me know – just to represent the family."

"It was a last-minute decision, and we just went down to the court house. We broke the news to Phil at a neighborhood pot-luck dinner, and that turned out to be our reception…."

"Yeah, and this is our honeymoon trip," Eric laughed.

"Well, you wouldn't have much privacy, but you can stay here with me if you want. You're sitting on the hideaway bed right now!"

"That would be the best wedding present you could give us, Lorraine. Thanks…."

"Nonsense. I'm taking you both out to dinner tonight, and I hope they have some champagne. So let's make up the bed, and you can change if you want to. But nobody gets dressed up at the seafood house next to the marina here. We can walk over."

The Fish House was the perfect place for weary travelers and people like Lorraine, who needed to unwind after a long day at work. They even dug up a bottle of champagne for the newlyweds, although most people were drinking beer. "To Jeff and Eric," Lorraine intoned, raising her glass. "May you have a long and happy life together!"

"Hear, hear!" Someone at the next table raised his glass, as the two kissed. A few others turned away, embarrassed or disapproving, but it didn't dampen their spirits.

—

"I'm sorry for some people's reaction to the two of you, Jeff," Lorraine apologized, as they walked back to her condo after dinner.

"We're used to it," Eric smiled, sadly. "This *is* the South, after all."

"That's no excuse," Lorraine said. "It's legal now!"

"It's actually a bit easier to live in Asheville," Jeff explained. "It's kind of like New York City, but on a smaller scale. Anything goes, and nobody pays any attention to anyone else. *Chacun à son goût!* To each his own...."

"Except at the topless parade every summer," Eric laughed. "Scores of women march topless down Patton Avenue, and the men line up to watch and take pictures. It's really just exhibitionism, since it's not illegal for women to go topless in public in Asheville, anyway."

"They must have started doing that after I left," Lorraine said. "It sounds like I've missed all the fun!"

"I'll let you know the date this year, and you can come and march, too!"

"No, thanks, but I might come and watch it. Maybe Karl would come with me...."

"Who's Karl?" Jeff perked up. His sister had never mentioned anyone before.

"Oh, just a guy I'm dating. His name is Karl Schmidt, and he's a defense lawyer for the county where I work. Depending on how long you can stay, maybe he would join us for some sightseeing or dinner. I don't know what his plans are this weekend though…."

"I'd be willing to bet that his plans involve you, Lorraine." Jeff raised an eyebrow. "As your older brother, I think I'd better meet this guy. Especially in our Daddy's absence…."

"I can live with that, but I just have one request. Don't tell Phil about Karl yet. My relationship with him might not last, and there's no point getting Phil in a tizzy over it."

"Okay, but I think you overestimate Phil's interest in who you're dating, little sis!"

—

Jeff and Eric stayed an extra day with Lorraine, just so they could meet her boyfriend Karl. He joined them for a morning of sightseeing in Wilmington, and an afternoon at Wrightsville Beach. July was perfect beach weather there, and Jeff was glad for an opportunity to talk to Karl alone while Lorraine and Eric were still in the water. "So, how long have you and Lorraine been dating, Karl?"

"Why do I feel as though I'm being grilled? *I'm* usually the one who asks the questions!"

"You don't have anything to hide, do you…? Just kidding, but I do feel kind of protective of my little sister. Our parents are both dead."

"I know, and I'm sorry. Lorraine and I met some years ago, when we were working the same case. She evaluated the suspect as competent to stand trial, and I defended him – unsuccessfully, as it turned out. After we got to know each other, we started dating. She's a special lady, in every sense of the word."

"I agree, and I wouldn't want to see her get hurt."

"She won't, if I have anything to say about it, Jeff."

"Thanks, Karl. I won't tell her that we had this conversation. She'd never speak to me again…."

"I know what you mean. She values her independence…."

Lorraine and Eric ran back to where Karl and Jeff were sitting on the beach blanket. "What have you two guys been talking about?" she asked, casually.

"Nothing earthshaking," Jeff replied. Karl was telling me about his job as a public defender."

"Not very exciting, I'm afraid," Karl shrugged.

"Neither is teaching, most of the time," Jeff acknowledged, and Eric agreed.

"I could say the same about mine," Lorraine smiled, "but it pays the bills."

"I'll drink to that." Karl got up and stretched. "How about some drinks from the vendor over there?"

"I'll have ginger ale," Lorraine said, and Jeff seconded it.

"I'll help carry," Eric offered, and the two of them left.

"So," Jeff broke the silence. "How do you feel about Karl?"

"I'm not as madly in love as you and Eric are," she laughed.

"You didn't answer my question." Jeff looked at her directly.

"Karl is one of the good guys," Lorraine said, "and there aren't that many around."

"Like Phil?"

"Yes, and like you, big brother."

"You haven't *always* been attracted to good guys, though."

"I'm changing, now that I'm thirty. Maybe seeing the error of my ways."

"Too late for Phil, unfortunately…."

"…Are Phil and Nora still seeing each other?"

"Yes, they are. In fact, she moved in with him recently – into his family's home, next to ours."

"I'm glad he's happy, and that you are, too, Jeff. Don't tell him I asked about Nora, though…."

"I won't, but why not?"

"I just don't want him to know that I still think about him, that's all."

"It might not be too late for him to know that, Lorraine."

"Yes, it is. He's moved on, and so have I. And it's for the best, for both of us."

"He and Nora are happy together – I know that much, but I think he'll always love you, too, Lorraine."

"I know, but it never would have worked out for us, Jeff. He belongs in Asheville, and I belong here in Wilmington. At least that's not a problem for Karl."

"There's more to love than agreeing on where to live, Lorraine. If Eric wanted to move, I would definitely consider it."

"That's what makes the two of us different, Jeff. I've established my life here, and if that means I stay single – then so be it."

"Then I don't think you really love Phil anymore, and maybe you don't feel that way about Karl, either. Just think about it…."

"I will, and I'm glad we had this talk…in person. I wish you and Eric every happiness, Jeff."

9

Sister Evelyn was back in Cullowhee, North Carolina, from her summer travels to see her family out west. She was anxious to start the fall semester at WCU, and came knocking on Amelia's office door on the morning of their departmental meeting. "Anybody home? Amelia?"

"You know that my office door would be open if I were here, Evelyn!" Amelia walked up behind her, key in hand. "Did they move the meeting up, and not let me know? Adjuncts aren't considered important members of the department – I should know that by now…."

"That's not true, Amelia. Nobody else could teach your French classes if you weren't here."

"Maybe not, but our new department head had no qualms about asking me to teach some of his beginning-*German* classes this fall, since he'll frequently be tied up in meetings with other department heads."

"What…? Did you say yes?"

"Come in my office for a minute, and I'll tell you. Otherwise it'll be all over the campus by noon." She closed the door after Evelyn came in and sat in her only other chair. "I told him no. It's been almost fifteen years since I finished my Masters in German, and I've only ever taught French, anyway. German grammar is much harder, and mine's rusty. I don't think it's fair to students for their teacher to be only one step ahead of them in class. I'd have to relearn the grammar before I could teach it!"

"But you said that you and Jack spent three years in Germany in the late 1990s. Didn't you speak German then?"

"I was working for the U.S. Government, so I interacted with Americans all day long – in English. We had German neighbors, and we traveled, but conversational German is different from teaching the grammar. Besides, we Americans don't even know our *own* grammar. How many people know when to use *who* or *whom*, and why?"

"I do…."

"Of course, but you're a linguist and a language teacher, not the man on the street – or even the nun on the street!"

"I admire you for turning down the chance to earn more money, but let's go get a cup of coffee before our meeting starts at 10:00. I'm beginning to wilt, after just one cup so far."

"Okay. The Coffee Cup across the street? Maybe they have bagels today, too. I had to leave home too early for breakfast. A full hour on the road to drive here is starting to get to me, after last school year. My whole salary went into my gas tank!"

"Ask the new department head to put you in for a raise. He'll be anxious to keep all his teachers happy and on the job."

"Except me, after I turned him down on his request to teach German, too, and double my course load. They don't pay me enough per course for all that extra work."

"I hear you, Amelia, and you don't get benefits, either, since you're part-time. Let's change the subject, and just relax with a cup of coffee."

—

The Coffee Cup wasn't very busy, since the semester hadn't formally begun yet.

"I wish it were this laid-back *all* the time, Evelyn. Nobody in a hurry to get to class, or any last-minute studying for exams. Sometimes the anxiety-level is through the roof in here. Today is the calm before the storm."

"I actually like it *better* when it's full of people, Amelia. Maybe that's because I'm alone at home most of the time. Sister Agnes pretty much stays to herself, when she's even there. That's probably not what our motherhouse had in mind when they paired us up here. We were meant to live in a community of our sisters. That's why we joined the order."

"I'm not alone at home – I have Jack and Autumn. Even when Jack isn't there, Autumn always welcomes me when I get home. But I still rely on *you* here on campus, Evelyn. I can talk to you about church-related stuff, too, and I know you'll understand. Like when I felt alienated from God, and you encouraged me to work my way back. You got me thinking about the real meaning of life, and it has nothing to do with my job. It's about my relationships with people like you, and my family, and my friends at church. I didn't really have a special friend in Maryland, until Jack came along. Now they're popping up all over the place here!"

—

Amelia got to thinking some more about their first year in North Carolina, and realized that another vocal group had also played an important part in her life here. She had always loved to sing, and had even joined the German-American Community Choir (GACC) while they were in Wiesbaden for three years. It was actually a chorus, but the German language didn't distinguish between a choir and a chorus – they were both called *ein Chor*. In any case, she really missed performing the Singing Christmas Tree concert with them every year. So last December she and Jack went to hear the Asheville Choral Society's (ACS) Christmas concert, and were blown away!

The chorus of about 150 singers had processed down both aisles of the darkened church, carrying lighted candles and singing Randall Thompson's <u>Alleluja</u>, *a cappella.* It was the same hymn that the GACC had used for its opener, and Amelia got goose-bumps. The ACS singers proceeded onto the stage, and finished the hymn in place on the risers. The rest of the concert was a mix of classical and traditional Christmas music from around the world, many pieces sung in their original languages. It was just the sort of challenge that Amelia wanted, and she joined the group after barely passing her audition with the director.

She had never been required to audition for any chorus she had ever joined, and she was quite nervous. She had been allowed to choose a Christmas carol to sing, and she gave the sheet music to the accompanist that day.

It was <u>Angels We Have Heard on High</u>, an 18th century French carol, and the director listened intently as she sang. Amelia wasn't a voice-trained soprano and when she was asked to sight-read an unfamiliar piece of music, she failed miserably. The director must have heard some degree of potential in her voice, however, because when the audition ended Amelia was welcomed into the group with enthusiasm.

Amelia's three new friends – Annie, Trish, and Evelyn – all came to hear the ACS sing various concerts while she was a member of the group. Annie always came on the Deerfield shuttle bus, Trish came at the last minute when her work schedule permitted, and Evelyn stayed with Amelia and Jack for several concert weekends. Knowing someone in the audience made all the difference in the world to Amelia, as when other members of her church choir and sometimes even the choir director herself showed up.

—

It was also during this period of high productivity in Amelia's life that Annie began to suspect that her friend had truly lost her mind. What woman with half a brain would take on another non-paying job when her available time and money were already stretched to the limit? Amelia's church of St. Eugene was asking for volunteers to tutor students of ESL (English as a Second Language).

The parish had a high percentage of Hispanic members, and many of them wanted to improve their English so that they could qualify for a better job. Amelia decided to help, and ended up tutoring four students – consecutively – who lived near her. The first was a middle-aged woman who wanted to pass her U.S. citizenship exam, and Amelia drilled her on the 100 possible questions she would encounter on the exam, using flash cards. The second was a young man who wanted to become a representative for a company that sold hair products. Amelia listened as he practiced his English presentation, and helped him with grammar and pronunciation. The third was a young woman who was so grateful for the help that she invited Amelia and Jack to her wedding.

The Hispanic wedding was a revelation to them – from the ceremony to the reception…that went on for hours before the bride and groom even arrived! They had been looking forward to the wedding cake, but finally finished their tacos and rice and had to leave before the newlyweds even made their appearance. The fourth student was a young wife and mother, whose baby girl slept while they did battle with the compound tenses in English. How do you explain a construction such as, "We *would have stayed* at the reception, if we *had* only *known* that the cake *was to be served* soon"?

It's a well-known fact that most people don't know the rules of their own language's grammar. They just grow up hearing their native language being spoken by those around them, and they imitate what they hear.

They don't have that advantage when they study a foreign language, however, so they have to learn the rules – conjugations, declensions, and genders of nouns. German nouns each have one of three genders (masculine, feminine, or neuter). Luckily, English language nouns all have the same gender – neuter. Thus the article "the" can be used with every noun in English. On the other hand, this makes it much easier to *teach* a foreign language than it is to teach your own. You have to learn the rules yourself, before you can speak it well. Then it's a breeze to pass that knowledge on.

———

Phil and Nora had been living together in Phil's house all summer, and batting around an idea with Jeff and Eric for a memorial service for all four of both Phil's and Jeff's parents. It had been a year since Phil's mother Alice had died, the last of the four, and it just seemed like the right time to remember all of them together. "And it'll give our relatives and friends a chance to get to know Eric and Nora," Jeff added, glancing at his new husband, Eric. He still couldn't believe they were really married, and that it was actually legal, too.

"This time the gathering afterwards will be at our house, though," Phil said, "since my mother was the last one to pass." Alice's spirit felt honored to be singled out by her son and his girlfriend. She remembered how kind Nora had been to her in her final days, as her nurse.

"Do you think Lorraine will come, Jeff?" Phil asked. "You've seen her more recently than I have."

"I'm sure she will, Phil. Why don't you call her? She can stay in her old room at home, if she wants to. You know, she really loved your mother…and you, too."

"I know…. Did you tell her that Nora moved in with me here?"

"Yes. She was very happy for both of you…." Nora overheard the back-and-forth between the two friends, and wondered how Phil felt about Lorraine now. She knew that Phil was once very much in love with Lorraine, and that they had known each other since childhood. How could she compete with that? She had only known Phil for a short time – not much more than a year. Now Lorraine would most likely be coming for the memorial service that included her own parents. Nora remembered meeting her at Alice's funeral – and she also remembered how beautiful she was….

The only thing that gave her hope was that Lorraine had been the one to break it off with Phil – he had told Nora so. Lorraine wanted to stay in Wilmington, and Phil felt the same way about West Asheville. But what if Lorraine had changed her mind? What if she tells Phil that now she is willing to move, and that she wants him back? This memorial service could be a defining moment for all of them, and Nora could find herself on the losing side.

10

Phil called Lorraine from his office at the Asheville hotel where he worked. He wasn't sure why, but he didn't want Nora to hear his conversation with her. She might get the wrong idea. "Lorraine, it's Phil. Can you talk for a minute?"

"Hi, Phil. Sure – I just finished my last interview of the day…. To what do I owe the honor of a phone call? Is everything okay?"

"Everybody's fine here, and I just wanted to extend a personal invitation to you, Lorraine."

"I'm all ears…."

"Jeff and I have decided to hold a memorial service for our four parents together. It's been a year since my mother's funeral, and we want to honor all of them. They were such good friends – and neighbors, too, of course."

"That's a great idea! What's the date?"

"September 23rd – it's a Saturday. Jeff says that you can stay with him and Eric."

"Well, it's a cinch I won't be staying with *you*, Phil, the way I did after your mother Alice died. I don't think that Nora would approve…."

"Probably not. She knows how I felt about you then."

"Past tense?"

"Yes….   I wouldn't want to make her uncomfortable."

"Don't you get tired of always doing the right thing by everyone, Phil?"

"You never complained when we were together, Lorraine."

"I guess that's because *I* was the recipient of your gallantry then. Never mind…. I'll get in touch with Jeff and probably fly in, the night before. Thanks for the invitation, Phil. I'll see you then."

"It will be good to have you here, Lorraine…. Bye."

—

One down, quite a few more to go, Phil thought. Alicia had dropped off their thirteen-year-old son Derek for the weekend, so Phil decided to broach the subject with him first. "Hey, Derek! Want to go to a movie this afternoon? Your pick."

"Cool. I'll check what's playing."

"Before you get online, I want to tell you what Jeff and I are planning. We want to have a memorial service at the cemetery for his parents and mine. Would you like to come – with your Momma, of course?"

"Sure, but you'll have to ask *her*.... I can't believe that Grandma has been gone for a whole year now, Daddy. I really miss her!"

"Me, too, Derek. Do you still have that journal you gave her to write in, after she had her first stroke?"

"I do, and I'm so glad you gave it back to me after she died. I like to read what she wrote, and I write in it sometimes myself, too. It helps, when I've had a bad day at school."

"No doubt. Okay, find a movie, and let's go. We can stop for pizza on the way home, if you want to."

One superhero movie and a pepperoni pizza later, they were back at home relaxing.

"Daddy, could we go to Grandma's church tomorrow morning? I remember how she used to take me sometimes, before she got sick."

"Well, I guess so. I have to admit that I don't go very often – mainly just Christmas, and maybe Easter – but sure, let's go tomorrow."

It made them both think of Grandma Alice when they walked into St. Eugene Church – the gathering space, Father Pat celebrating the Mass, and afterwards saying hello to Amelia Flynn as she was leaving the choir area. "You know, Amelia sang for Grandma Alice's funeral a year ago, Derek."

"Then she came to your house afterwards, right, Daddy?"

"That's right, Derek," Amelia smiled. "And I was so inspired when you read something from her journal during the service – how she wanted everyone to celebrate her life instead of mourning her death."

"And that's just what we're going to do in a few weeks, Amelia," Phil jumped in. Would you and Jack like to join us for a memorial service, for my parents and also Jeff's parents? They were all friends, and after the service we'll all meet at my house and celebrate their extraordinary lives."

"I'd love to, and I know that Jack would, too. You can let us know the details, Phil. I have to run now, but I'm so glad I saw you two today. I'll talk to you again soon, Derek!"

Phil's occasional weekends with Derek were always over too soon, and Alicia's knock on his door that Sunday afternoon meant that it was time to say goodbye again. "Alicia – come in," Phil gestured to her. "Derek, your Momma's here. Go up and collect all your stuff. Check the bathroom to be sure you have everything, and I'll ask her about the memorial service."

"Another memorial service? Who is this one for?"

"For both Jeff's and my parents combined – all four together. It will be on September 23rd, a Saturday, and we'd like you and Derek to come to the cemetery and then back here afterwards to get together with everyone."

"Your mother was always good to me, Phil. Of course I'll bring Derek over for the service. Is Nora here?"

"No, she's working a day shift lately. You know how it is with nurses…."

"Yes, and I think it's odd how you keep gravitating toward nurses – first me, and now Nora. Is it our nurturing personalities?"

"Maybe nurses are just sexy – I don't know."

Phil realized that he shouldn't be teasing Alicia like that. She might take it seriously. But she must know that he only had eyes for Nora now…. "Are you dating anyone, Alicia?"

"Me? When would I have time to date? The hospital keeps me pretty busy."

"I'm sure Nora would sympathize with you. Maybe you'll get a chance to talk to her after the service."

"I'll look forward to it." *Why would I want to talk about nursing when I get a day off? Especially with a kid like her, who's probably ten years younger than me….* "Come on, Derek! Let's hit the road."

"I'll see you and your Momma at the memorial service, Derek. Tell her about the movie we saw yesterday."

"Nah…she wouldn't have liked it, Daddy."

"Hey, kid! You might be surprised!" Alicia ruffed up his hair on the way out.

"Thanks, Alicia," Phil said, touching her arm as they left. "I'll call you about the schedule, as soon as we decide."

"No rush. I'll put in for the whole day off."

—

Jeff picked up his sister Lorraine at the Asheville Regional Airport, the night before the memorial service. She was exhausted after a layover in Charlotte when she changed planes. Karl was by her side, which came as a total surprise to Jeff, and Lorraine enjoyed the shocked look on her brother's face. "Turnabout is fair play!" she laughed. "Remember when you and Eric showed up on my doorstep unannounced, earlier this summer?" Karl was embarrassed, not having known that Jeff wasn't expecting him.

"That's my sister for you," Jeff smiled, welcoming Karl with a handshake. "Always keep 'em guessing…. How are you, Karl?"

"Apologetic…but glad to be here. Where's that new husband of yours?"

"Eric stayed behind to take care of last-minute details, like getting Lorraine's room ready. I presume you'll be sharing it, Karl, or else there's always my old room down the hall."

Karl was smart enough to defer that decision to Lorraine, since they were talking about the house she grew up in. She didn't hesitate. "There's no sense in making up two beds," she said with a straight face, and that was that.

It was still light as they drove home from the airport, and Lorraine played tour guide for Karl, who had never been to western North Carolina.

He asked questions about things she took for granted, like the size of Asheville and its claim to fame. Despite living on the coast now, she couldn't help the feeling of pride in her voice as she told him about the Biltmore Estate and the Grove Park Inn, which was built by Mr. Vanderbilt's rival, Mr. Grove, over a hundred years ago. Karl was surprised when Lorraine disclosed that her family home was in the small community of West Asheville, not in Asheville itself, however.

"Hey, Eric!" Karl was beginning to enjoy startling people with his unexpected presence, when he walked in with Lorraine.

"Welcome…both of you! It feels odd to say 'welcome,' when this is *your* house, though, Lorraine," Eric laughed, giving her a hug.

"Not anymore, it isn't. Now it belongs to you and Jeff, and I'm sure that our parents would be very proud that the two of you decided to stay here."

"We didn't plan a big dinner tonight," Eric apologized. "I just made some soup and sandwiches, before we all crash – especially the travelers."

"You got that right, Eric!" Karl said. "What's the schedule for the service tomorrow? Can we sleep late…?"

"We got you covered," Jeff jumped in. "The memorial service won't start until early afternoon, and then we're hoping that everyone will come back to Phil's house to socialize for a while. Some neighbors have already said that they'll bring food and drinks."

"I miss that sense of belonging to a neighborhood," Lorraine sighed. "Living in a condo just isn't the same. Nobody really cares about anyone else, and I hardly ever see the other residents, anyway. Then, before you know it, someone moves out and someone else moves in! There's no continuity, like there is here."

It wasn't long after their supper that everyone decided to call it a day. Jeff and Eric had been busy with preparations for the next day, and Lorraine and Karl were done in by their long day of travel. "You guys can use the hall bathroom, Lorraine," Jeff said. "We have our own in Momma and Daddy's room, as I'm sure you remember."

"Do I ever! I always wanted to soak in their tub, when I was a teenager…. Goodnight, Jeff."

"Sleep as late as you want, Lorraine. Coffee will be ready whenever you get up."

"I could get used to this," she said to Karl, when she finally climbed into the double bed with him.

"It's smaller than your bed, Lorraine, but that just means that you're closer to me all night. I like going to sleep with my arms around you."

"I keep expecting my mother to find us in bed together here – like Romeo and Juliet. And we both know how *that* ended!"

"But we're not in our teens anymore, Lorraine. We're both over thirty, and our lives are meant for us to enjoy right now, however we want…."

"I wish I were as certain about my life as you seem to be, Karl."

11

The four spirits who were the honorees of the memorial service were already waiting at the cemetery on Saturday for it to begin. They watched as Phil directed its employees in the placement of the folding chairs and the podium for the speakers. Alice's spirit was particularly nervous when it came to her son Phil. Would there be fireworks when Lorraine showed up with Karl in tow? "Don't worry," Daniel's spirit tried to comfort his wife. "Phil can handle it. He's used to dealing with sticky situations at the hotel he manages."

Friends and neighbors began to arrive, and Phil was wondering what was keeping Jeff. He assumed that Lorraine had flown in last night, but he hadn't seen or heard from her. Nora had made sure that the house was ready for guests before she left, and she was now seated in the front row of chairs while Phil fiddled with the sound equipment.

Nora turned to greet various neighbors she had met since moving in with Phil over the summer, but she still felt like an interloper somehow. At least Eric and Jeff were married now, but Nora wasn't sure *what* her own status was…in Phil's eyes.

"Nora looks lost," Alice's spirit commented to her husband Daniel. "I do wish that Phil would shit or get off the pot!"

"Alice! I'm shocked to hear you talk like that!"

"Why? You say that all the time!"

"Yes, but men are expected to be more…candid than women."

"Maybe it's time for women to do the same…. Oh, look! It's that new couple in the neighborhood – Amelia and Jack. She sang at my funeral, you know. How nice of them to come!"

——

Nora was pleased to see the Flynns, too. She got up and went over to welcome them personally. "Amelia, Jack! I'm so glad you came. Everyone else here has been living in the neighborhood forever!"

"Eric hasn't. Where *are* Jeff and Eric, by the way? Shouldn't Jeff be helping Phil?" Amelia asked, and Nora agreed.

"I think that Jeff's sister Lorraine flew in for the service, but we haven't seen her yet." Nora had met Lorraine right before Alice's funeral a year ago, when Phil was still hoping to convince her to move back to West Asheville. That hadn't happened, but Nora remembered how Phil and Lorraine had held hands and looked at each other so lovingly then – the same way Phil looked at Nora now. Could she ever trust such changeable feelings in him?

"Are you and Jack coming to our house afterwards, Amelia? I know that Phil hopes you will."

"We wouldn't want to intrude," she replied.

"Don't be foolish! It would be a good opportunity for you to meet some more of your neighbors here, and I'm hoping to do the same."

"Could you use a bottle or two of Biltmore wine, Nora?" Jack settled the issue.

"That would be great, Jack. We'll see you two later, then." Nora sat back down, preferring to stay in the background, but just then Alicia and Derek arrived and sat down behind Nora, making their presence known.

"Hello, Nora," Alicia said, as formally as she knew how to be. Nora turned around, and smiled at Derek.

"Hi…! Go up and see if your Daddy needs any help, Derek," Nora encouraged him, and then resigned herself to dealing with Alicia on her own.

"Phil thought we might want to talk about nursing." Alicia rolled her eyes. "But that's the last thing I want to discuss on my day off."

"I know how you feel, even though some patients are hard to banish from your thoughts when you're not there."

"Yeah. Some people are hard to forget…like Phil." Alicia wished she could take that back, but it was too late.

"I know I'm very lucky to have him Alicia, but I never thought I was taking him away from *you*…."

"You didn't, Nora. It's all ancient history, but sometimes I regret giving him up…you know?"

"I do. We all have regrets, but you have Derek, don't forget. He'll always be yours, no matter how old he is."

"And Phil's, too. That's what hurts sometimes…." Nora didn't know how to respond to that, but a commotion behind them pre-empted their conversation.

—

Jeff had arrived, escorting his sister Lorraine. They were followed by Eric, and another man that nobody recognized. Jeff and Lorraine went right up to Phil and Derek at the podium, and she hugged them both warmly. Then she took Phil by the hand and they walked back to where Eric and Karl were sitting. "Phil, this is my good friend, Karl Schmidt. He's a defense attorney for the county where I work." Karl stood up and the two men shook hands. He was well aware of what Phil had once meant to Lorraine.

"I'm pleased to meet you, Karl, and I'm glad you could accompany Lorraine on this special weekend," Phil said. Karl appeared to be a serious young man in his thirties, and he nodded to Phil as he sat back down next to Eric. Lorraine joined Nora in the front row, and greeted her in a friendly manner. Derek rejoined his mother Alicia, and the crowd settled down. Phil stepped up to the microphone, and smiled at all the familiar faces who were there to honor his parents and Jeff's. The memorial service was about to begin.

"Thank you all for coming today to celebrate the lives of my parents, Alice and Daniel Clark, and Jeff's parents, Jane and Robert Walker. My mother Alice was the last to leave us, just one year ago, but I'm quite sure that all four of their spirits are with us here today. They must be very proud when they witness the outpouring of our love for them – from family members, old and new friends, and neighbors. I just want my parents to know that I plan to live in their house, right here in West Asheville, for the rest of my days.

"And don't worry, Momma – I'll take care of your apple trees, and maybe Nora will make us a pie or some apple sauce every once in a while." Nora blushed, and Lorraine just smiled. "And now it's Jeff's turn to talk about *his* parents." Jeff traded places with Phil and took a deep breath. He was a teacher but he wasn't used to talking to *this* many people at a time.

"Most of you know that Phil and I have been best friends since we were little, growing up right next door to each other. He knew my family, and I knew his. Ever since before my parents died, I knew that I wanted to keep living in their house – in the neighborhood that I love. When Eric and I got married, it was with the understanding that we would spend our life together here. I want to thank all of you for welcoming Eric, and for your acceptance of us as a married couple. I only hope that my parents are as proud of me now, as they always were when I was little."

Although it was a cloudy day, the sun broke through dramatically as soon as Jeff finished speaking, and everyone smiled at him as they clapped. The spirits of their four parents looked at each other, wondering who had that much clout with God – but it remained a mystery. Maybe Jeff's guardian angel had interceded on his behalf. Even the pastor of St. Eugene Church, whom Phil had asked to say a few words and lead the prayer at the end of the service, had no clue what it all meant. It certainly became a topic of conversation at the gathering that followed, however.

—

Phil's house was packed to the gills before long, and there was an abundance of food and drink. It was a bit too crowded and loud for Amelia and Jack, however, and they only stayed long enough to have something to drink before walking home. The memorial service itself had been more their speed, but they did enjoy meeting Lorraine's boyfriend Karl at the gathering afterwards.

"I guess we can forget about Lorraine and Phil ever getting back together," Jack teased.

"Oh, I don't know. It's not over till it's over…which usually means until someone gets married."

"But even then, you can't just turn off your feelings."

"Unless you can change a lover into a friend…." Amelia liked having the last word, even though they were both wondering whether their spouse was speaking from experience.

Nora didn't know everyone who was there, so Phil tried to keep her in his sights and introduce her around. It was overwhelming for her, though, and after a while she just busied herself in the kitchen when a platter need to be replenished. Before Amelia left, she found Nora there to say thank you for her hospitality.

"I'm happy you came, Amelia. At least now I'm not the only new kid on the block."

"Don't forget Karl. He's definitely a fish out of water here, but judging from his interaction with Lorraine I'd say that they care about each other very much."

"I'm glad – I like Lorraine…as a person."

"Just not as Phil's girlfriend anymore…."

Nora had to laugh. "You help me to see things more clearly, Amelia. I hope we can be friends."

"I need friends as much as you do, Nora."

—

Phil was flitting around, trying to talk to everyone, when he noticed Lorraine standing alone with a drink in her hand. "Where's your knight in shining armor?" he joked.

"Karl? He excused himself to find the bathroom."

"I'm so happy you're both here, Lorraine. Karl seems like a nice guy."

"He is – one of the best – like you, Phil."

"Neither one of us was ever much for playing the field, Lorraine. Now it seems like each of us has found someone special that checks our most important boxes."

"You always *were* a romantic, Phil!" she laughed. "But you're right. Karl likes Wilmington as much as I do. We can just be ourselves around each other."

"Am I interrupting anything?" Karl asked, when he returned.

"I just wanted to tell Lorraine that maybe the four of us could be long-distance friends down the road. Nora and I might want to see the coast together sometime, or you and Lorraine might like to explore the Blue Ridge Mountains. Let's not lose touch after you leave – that's all I'm saying."

"That's okay by me, Phil. I don't know much about this area at all, so Lorraine can be my guide. I'm sure she'll want to visit Jeff and Eric from time to time, too. Family is important…."

"Did you hear that, Robert?" Jane's spirit drew his attention to the conversation between Phil and Karl. "Karl thinks that it's important for Lorraine to keep in touch with her brother Jeff. Maybe this guy Karl will be good for our daughter, after all."

"I hope so, Jane, since there's not a damn thing we can do about it anymore, if he's not…."

12

Phil noticed that Alicia and Derek were getting ready to leave the gathering and drive back to Waynesville, so he walked over to them. "I really miss Grandma, Daddy," Derek gave Phil a hug, "especially when I'm here in her house."

"Me, too, Derek, but it helps me remember the good times with her. I want you to know that you're always welcome to visit me here." Phil glanced at Alicia, to see her reaction to his invitation, but she didn't seem to be objecting.

"Thanks for wanting us to come to the memorial service, Phil. It was important for Derek to be here."

"It was meaningful for all of us, Alicia, and Derek is the link that connects us all now. I'll see you both again soon…."

Nora hadn't wanted to intrude, but now she stood next to Phil as they watched Derek and Alicia get into their car. Derek turned at the last minute and flashed Phil the sign of peace through the open car window as they drove off, a smile on his face.

"You're so lucky to have him, Phil," she said, taking his hand as they stood in the doorway.

"I know, and to have you as well makes me the luckiest guy in the world, Nora…."

—

But Nora and Phil really didn't belong to each other…not really, even though she lived with him in his house. Her night shift at the hospital lately meant that their time at home together didn't amount to much, unless they happened to have the same day off. It was on one of those rare Sunday afternoons that they took advantage of the lovely autumn weather to explore the Biltmore Estate once again, and they had a chance to talk about their life together. They had taken a picnic lunch in backpacks, and hiked around a large pond to a scenic spot where they could spread a blanket within sight of the mansion on a nearby hilltop.

"Here's one of the bottles of Biltmore wine that Jack brought to the get-together after the memorial service, Nora, and we don't even have to share it with anyone now."

"It's appropriate that we should drink it here, too, even if it's not strictly allowed. Which one is it?"

"The Riesling. I even packed some glasses, while you were choosing our picnic food."

"Mmm…my favorite wine, and it'll go great with the baguette and cheeses I brought. We should do this more often, Phil."

"I'd love to, if we could ever sync up our work schedules. What are the chances you could go back on a day shift at the hospital, so we could spend our evenings together and maybe even an occasional weekend?"

"I promise to talk to my supervisor about it – next week. How's that?"

"I'll drink to that! Get out the glasses while I open this…. Here's to more time like this together, pretending that we're the invited guests of George Vanderbilt…"

"killing time on the grounds, until we go back into the mansion to change for dinner in the formal dining room…"

"along with all his other friends from New York City who are spending the weekend here with George and his wife – what's-her-name. May I have a refill, please, Monsieur?"

"By all means, Mademoiselle – on one condition."

"And what is that, pray tell?"

"That you consent to marry me, Nora…." He put down the bottle and took the velvet box out of his backpack. Kneeling up on one knee, he opened it to reveal a marquise-diamond-solitaire engagement ring. "I've loved you ever since you came to take care of my mother at home, Nora. I just didn't realize it until after she died, and I thought I had lost you…."

"I loved you then, too, Phil, and I still do now. So my answer is yes, I would marry you today if I could!" She cried happy tears as he slipped the ring on her finger, and then he remembered his promise to refill her glass!

"Now we can drink to our married life together – only if you intend to keep *your* promise," he laughed, but Nora was drawing a blank. "To talk to your supervisor next week!" She nodded, but all she could do then was stare at the exquisite ring on her finger, and kiss her new fiancé.

—

"I'm allowed to change my shift when we get married, Phil! That will give them enough time to rearrange the master schedule at the hospital. So let's make our plans right away! I don't want to wait, in any case…."

"Okay, but hold your horses, Nora! This is already October, so how about November?"

"November…?   Let's get married on Thanksgiving, Phil! Then we'll never forget our anniversary, and we'll always celebrate with a turkey dinner!"

Phil couldn't help but smile, at the exuberance of her youth. To her, nothing was impossible, or even difficult. If she could dream it, she could do it! "But where, Nora? Who would perform a wedding ceremony on a holiday?"

"The pastor at your church, of course! What else does he have to do on Thanksgiving, besides go to someone's house for dinner? This way we can invite him to *our* house, after the ceremony. I'll put the turkey in the oven before we go to church – it'll be perfect! You're a parishioner at St. Eugene, right?"

"Well,   theoretically,   because   of   my mother…."

"Good enough. He wouldn't say no to one of his parishioners, especially after you just had him speak at the memorial service…."

"Okay, I'll ask him."

"And I'll come with you. That'll cinch it."

"I love you, Nora! You make me feel like I can do anything I set my mind to, as long as you're with me."

"Funny…I feel the same way about you, Phil."

—

Father Pat agreed to their plan – there was no reason not to. But he had to decline their dinner invitation for afterwards, since his extended family would have protested. That only left the question of who would be their witnesses, and Nora already knew who she wanted to ask. She called her new friend, Amelia. "You're not going to believe this," Nora began.

"You're not working nights anymore…."

"Close…. Phil asked me to marry him, but he wants me to go back on the day shift."

"Now *there's* an incentive if I ever heard one! I assume you said yes!"

"I did, and my supervisor says I can make the switch as soon as we're married! That's where *you* come in…."

"Me? *I* can't perform the ceremony!"

"No, but you can be my matron of honor, Amelia. Please say you will – it would mean such a lot to me. We outsiders have to stick together!"

"First of all, congratulations to both of you! When and where will the wedding be?"

"At St. Eugene Church, on this Thanksgiving Day – whatever date that is...."

"That's next month! You guys don't let any grass grow under your feet, do you!"

"What does *that* mean...?"

"Never mind. It's toward the end of November, so that's right around the corner. I'd love to be in your wedding, Nora – thank you! My boys alternate holidays with their father, so we'd be alone on Thanksgiving, anyway, this year. Do you have family coming?"

"No, I'm an only child and my parents are dead – Phil and I are alike in that way. Maybe that's why we understand each other so well. We'd just like a small wedding, but in church – it's what his mother would have wanted for him."

"Who's the best man?"

"Phil is figuring that out right now. I'll let you know. But don't buy a new dress, Amelia. I'm sure you already have something that's perfect. I wish *I* did...."

"I still have the white lace dress I wore when I married Jack a decade ago, Nora. I was thinner then, so it just might fit you. Let me know if you'd like to try it on."

———

There was no contest when it came to Phil's best man. It had to be his best friend, Jeff. They had grown up together, and still lived next door to each other. Jeff was also the first person that Phil wanted to tell about his engagement to Nora. "You'll be glad to know I finally did it, Jeff." Phil found him puttering around in his garage.

"What…quit your job?"

"No way! I'm going to need it now that I'm getting married!"

"I hope you mean to Nora…. Otherwise, I'm going to have to defend her honor by challenging you to a duel, and we both know who would come out on top of that one!"

"Of course it's Nora, you nitwit! And I want you to be my best man! Will you do it?"

"I don't know – my social calendar is pretty full, but I might be able to squeeze you in. When?"

"Thanksgiving Day – *this* Thanksgiving Day."

"You're in luck. All we have planned is a blowout turkey dinner, to which you and Nora are invited. Actually, Phil, I'd be honored to stand up for you, *and* we can all still have dinner together afterwards at our place."

"Thanks, man. You had me worried for a minute. Can we bring Amelia and Jack to dinner, too? Amelia is Nora's matron of honor, so she won't have time to cook."

"Eric is the chef at our house – and the more people around the table, the better he likes it. Luckily a turkey pretty much roasts itself, once you get it in the oven. Maybe we can get Jack to bring some bubbly from the Biltmore, and we won't care *what* time we eat after a few toasts! What about Derek, Phil? Have you told him yet?"

"He's next on my list. I'm sure he'll be with his mother for Thanksgiving dinner at her parents' house, but I would really like him to come to the wedding first."

"I don't envy you that conversation with Alicia, buddy. Not if she goes ballistic! Good luck…."

—

"Nora and I are getting married on Thanksgiving morning in Asheville, Alicia, and I really want Derek to be there.

"Can you spare him for a few hours, unless you'd like to bring him yourself and stay for the ceremony? I know you'll want him back for dinner with your parents later." There was silence at the other end of the line. Then…tentatively…

"Congratulations to both of you, Phil. I know that I was never really in the running, but I hope you'll be happy together. I don't think you really want me there, though…. My tears wouldn't be tears of joy, I'm afraid, and that wouldn't be fair to Derek. I'll drop him off at your house that morning, whenever you say. Can you get him back to my parents' house after the ceremony?"

"Whatever *you* say, Alicia. Thanks for understanding…."

Phil would have preferred to tell Derek in person about his plans with Nora, but he wasn't sure when he'd see his son next. As it turned out, Alicia beat him to it. "Momma told me you're getting married, Daddy – to Nora. That's cool...."

"I really wanted to tell you myself, but I had to clear it with your Momma for you to come to the wedding. I hope you want to...."

"Sure, Daddy! When is it?"

"Thanksgiving morning, at St. Eugene Church in Asheville. I hope that your Grandma Alice and Grandpa Daniel will be there in spirit, too."

"Did Momma make a stink about it...?"

"Only about it being on Thanksgiving. She'll drop you off here, and I'll get you back to her parents' house in time for your turkey dinner."

"Won't you and Nora celebrate Thanksgiving, Daddy?"

"Don't worry about *us*, Derek. Eric is inviting us back to their house after the ceremony for turkey and all the trimmings. In fact, he wants you to sit with him in church, since Jeff is going to be my best man."

"That'll be great! I wish I could spend the whole day with you guys...."

"Me, too, Derek, but it's your Momma's turn to have you with *them* this year."

"I hate being on a schedule like that! When can I make up my own mind about where I want to be?"

"When you're eighteen, I guess, so it'll be a while. I'm just glad she's letting you be at the ceremony, though. I need you to be there, Derek, and so does Nora. You're an important part of our little family."

"Thanks, Daddy. I wouldn't miss it, no matter what she says."

—

"Oh, my gosh, Amelia! Your wedding dress is drop-dead gorgeous!"

"Didn't your mother ever show you hers, Nora?"

"No, they got married at the court house, and then they died years later in a car accident. I was on my own by then, but I still miss them even now."

"Of course you do. If you would like to try on my dress, Nora, I would be honored, although I would never presume to take your mother's place."

Amelia's second wedding dress was of ivory lace, with bell sleeves and a plunging back that was considered avant-garde in the mid-1990s. The hem was cut longer in the back than the front, and was what used to be termed tea-length. The see-through lace bodice featured an under slip of ivory satin. All in all, it took Nora's breath away when she tried it on at Amelia's house that afternoon, without telling Phil what she was up to. "I love it!" she said, giving Amelia a hug that brought tears to her friend's eyes. Amelia had never had a daughter, but now she knew what that might have felt like.

"Let's go over to my dry cleaners together, Nora, and their tailor might want to take a little 'nip or a tuck' first, as they used to say. You're going to be a beautiful bride when Phil sees you walking down the aisle toward him!"

"Thank you so much, Amelia! Can I ask you something?"

"Of course, Sweetie – anything."

"Would you consider walking *with* me, down the aisle? I know that my parents would do it, if they were still here."

"Oh, thank God, Nora! I was dreading walking ahead of you by myself! I'm old enough to 'give you away,' though...."

"Don't worry – I'm old enough to give myself away, don't you think?"

"Definitely, and so is Phil!" she laughed.

—

Nora and Phil didn't want to have a big wedding, so they only invited close friends and neighbors. Neither one of them had any family to speak of, and everyone who came to the ceremony had their own Thanksgiving dinner to fix or attend afterwards. It was an inexpensive way to get married, and celebrate the holiday at the same time. No lavish reception that they'd be paying for in the years to come. They could save their money for some sort of honeymoon trip instead. It made perfect sense to both of them.

The only thing that Nora wanted to keep a secret from Phil was her wedding dress, so Amelia picked it up after it was altered and kept it at her house until that morning. The wedding was at twelve noon, so Nora walked over to Amelia's house to change and do her hair and makeup on Thursday morning. Meanwhile, Phil was waiting for Alicia to drop Derek off at his house. She didn't come in, thankfully, since neither one of them wanted to deal with the emotions that might suddenly emerge. Derek was all smiles in his only sports coat and tie, and Phil was very proud of him.

"You look great, Derek."

"So do you, Daddy. I don't think I've ever seen you in a suit…."

"Likewise. I must admit that I'm a bit nervous, though."

"Why? Where's Nora?"

"She's over at Amelia's house getting ready, since Amelia is her matron of honor. She said that they will drive her to church, so now it's just you and me, kid."

"What about Jeff and Eric?"

"They'll come as soon as Eric gets the turkey in the oven. We'd better get going now, so I can talk to Fr. Pat beforehand. Last minute stuff, you know…?"

"No, I don't, but he's pretty cool. And you need to calm down, Daddy…. You and Nora were meant for each other, whether you get married or not. And don't worry about Momma. She knows that, too, even though she'd probably never admit it. And she's stronger than you think – she has her life, and you have yours."

"Thanks, son. That does make me feel better…."

—

"Oh, my God, Nora!" Jack exclaimed as she came down the stairs, followed by Amelia. "That dress suits you beautifully…just as it did Amelia," he was quick to add. He already knew that she would be wearing it, but all he could think about was the day he married Amelia and saw it for the first time. Now his bride was wearing a hunter-green-lace dress, and acting very maternal toward Nora. He approved. "The florist just delivered the flowers, so let's see what they look like." Amelia and Jack had taken it upon themselves to provide the bridal bouquet, and corsages for Phil and the two witnesses.

Jack presented Nora with a small bouquet of red and white rosebuds, and Amelia with a wrist corsage to match. He would make sure that Phil and Jeff got their boutonnieres, too.

"I just texted Phil," Nora said, "and he's already at church, talking with Fr. Pat.

"So I guess it's safe for us to arrive and stay out of sight. I don't want him to see me ahead of time. Is that silly?"

"Not at all, Nora," Amelia smiled. "We want him to be surprised – and blown away! Let's go…."

Jack had plenty of room in the back seat for the bride, but Amelia thought of one more finishing touch. She pulled out one of the white rosebuds from her own corsage, and clipped it behind Nora's ear, making her look like a Spanish dancer. "Very festive," she laughed, and off they went.

Jack parked on the curved drive in front of the church, and Amelia took Nora to the ladies room to reconnoiter. Then he walked up to the altar and helped Phil and Jeff with their boutonnieres. Fr. Pat did his best to calm the boys down, as Jack joined Eric and Derek in the front row of pews. When Fr. Pat saw that the bride was in position at the back of the church, he signaled the organist to begin the wedding march. The small group of their friends and neighbors stood and turned to behold Nora walking proudly down the aisle on Amelia's arm.

Amelia's friend Trish was singing with the choir that day, and the two caught each other's eye and smiled. But the most wide-eyed look of love belonged to the groom, who couldn't believe his good fortune when he glimpsed his bride coming toward him as though the rest of the world didn't exist.

He reached out his hand to her when she arrived at the altar, and never let go. The ceremony went by in the blink of an eye – their vows, the rings, the readings, the homily, the hymns, and finally their first kiss as husband and wife.

Nora felt the presence of her parents' spirits throughout the ceremony, and of course the spirits of Phil's parents, Alice and Daniel, had already made their acquaintance beforehand. "Your daughter looks lovely," Alice remarked, "and our son Phil is a lucky man."

"It certainly took him long enough to realize it," Nora's mother said. "But I guess it's better late than never…."

"Now, ladies," Nora's father interjected, "the only thing that matters is that they're happy, and it looks to me like that's the case."

"I agree," Daniel chimed in. "If we weren't spirits, I would propose a toast, but the most we can do is watch as someone else does…."

After the rice was tossed on their way out, and the couple drove back home in Jack's car, however, the first toast had to wait until Phil delivered his son to Waynesville and the eager arms of Alicia and her parents. "I don't think I should come in, Derek. You can give them a blow-by-blow account of the ceremony, okay? I'm so glad you were there with us, though."

"For sure, Daddy! And Grandma Alice was there, too, holding my hand. I could feel how proud she was of you."

"See if your Momma will let you come for a visit with us soon, Derek. We might take a little honeymoon trip, but I'll call you when we get back."

"I love you both, Daddy, and I just want you and Nora to be happy."

"Then your wish has already come true, Derek. We couldn't be happier, and we love *you*, too! Have a Happy Thanksgiving, and give your Momma our best wishes. Now get in there, while there's still some turkey left!"

"Okay, and you do the same, Daddy."

—

When Phil got back to Jeff and Eric's house, the roasting turkey smelled delicious, and the party was in full swing. Jack popped the cork on a bottle of Biltmore's sparkling wine, and Nora ran into Phil's arms, as though she hadn't seen him in *forever*!

"I'd like to propose a toast," Jeff raised his glass as soon as everyone had been served, "to Mr. and Mrs. Nora & Phil Clark. May they live a long and happy life together right here in West Asheville, among all of us who love them!"

"Hear, hear!" they all shouted, draining their glasses.

"Now *who's* going to carve the turkey?" Eric laughed.

14

Nora and Phil left the Thanksgiving Day party fairly early, to spend their first night as husband and wife alone together in their house next door. "We could still go downtown, Nora, and spend our first night at the hotel where I work. I happen to know that the bridal suite is available, and it would be gratis for us…."

"We wouldn't really be alone, though. Everyone from the front desk, to room service, to the chambermaids would spread the word, and they'd all be smiling behind our backs. I'd much rather be with you here, in our bed, Phil. Now that I'm not on the night shift anymore, we can be together every night from now on – just like normal people."

"There was nothing normal about our love story, you're right, but at least it has a happy ending. So how about if we continue our happy ending here and now…?"

"Oops – wait a minute!   I forgot something…." Nora jumped out of bed, gloriously naked, and proceeded to light the half-dozen candles she had placed around the room before she left that morning. With the bedroom lights out, it looked like a fairyland and Phil was enchanted – with her, with their room, and with the sweet love they made until the wee hours.

———

"Good morning, Mrs. Clark." Phil joined her in the kitchen, where she was making coffee, and wrapped his arms around his bride. "How forward-thinking of you to suggest a wedding day at the beginning of a long holiday weekend!"

"Thank you, Mr. Clark, and when we have to go back to work, maybe they'll appreciate us even more than before."

"Let's go somewhere this weekend, Nora! Somewhere nobody knows us…. When do you go back to work?"

"Monday. My supervisor knows we just got married."

"I can pull rank at the hotel, and call in assistant-managers to cover for me until then, too. Have you ever been to Mount Pisgah, near the Blue Ridge Parkway?"

“I know where it is, but I’ve never had time off to explore that area – too busy supporting myself, I guess.”

“Well, we’re going to change all that, Nora, and what better opportunity than our honeymoon? Do you have hiking boots, by any chance?”

“Not really, but I do have those sturdy high-top sneakers. Would they do?”

“Let’s find out…. I’m going to make a call, and see if we can spend two nights at the Pisgah Inn on the Parkway. The colorful leaf season is already past and, if I have to, I’ll tell them that my hotel will recommend theirs to visitors, if they find us a room. What do you think?”

“I think that this is going to be an exciting honeymoon, but spent mostly outdoors instead of indoors….”

“Don’t worry, we’ll get back to our room with plenty of time for the indoor activities you have in mind.”

“If we have enough energy left…!”

“Since you’re only twenty-five, I wouldn’t worry. I have almost ten years on you, though.”

“I know, that’s why *you’re* the one I’m worried about, Phil!”

He couldn't let that comment slide. "Come here, you little minx, and we'll see who has more stamina!" That was just the reaction she was hoping to elicit, of course.

—

That afternoon they were packed and on their way, headed toward the nearby Blue Ridge Parkway that led to the Pisgah Inn. The speed limit on the Parkway was 25-45 miles per hour, probably to discourage its use by commuters. The section of the Parkway that passed through Asheville was capped at 25 mph, for that reason. It was meant to be for visitors and sightseers, who enjoyed its views of the nearby mountain ranges at lookout points. Motorcyclists were regular travelers on the Parkway, too, especially during the summer and on weekends.

In no time they had reached the Pisgah Inn. It was a clear and sunny afternoon, although Daylight Savings Time was no longer in effect, so it would be too late for anything but checking into their room and a short walk around the property. The view from the dining room was breathtaking for now, and they looked forward to having dinner there later. They would make a breakfast reservation for a table next to the floor-to-ceiling window that looked out over the valley, and the mountains in the distance.

"I love our room, Phil. The hotel is laid out like a high-class, country motel – each room is looking out over the same view as the restaurant next door.

"Can we just take a nap until it's time for dinner? The view here is dizzying!"

"Wait until we get to the top of Mount Pisgah tomorrow, Nora. Then you can talk about dizzying heights!"

"What…? We're going to *hike* up? Can we even see it from here?"

"There it is – the nearest peak to us. I haven't done it myself yet, so it'll be symbolic for us to do it together."

"Symbolic of what? Our insanity?"

"No – people like us hike up there all the time. It's not like Mt. Everest…. Mt. Pisgah has trails, I'm told, and places to stop along the way."

"Like restaurants?"

"More like benches. But it's only 1.6 miles to the summit, I hear. Since we start the climb at roughly 5,000 feet already, our ascent is only about 700 feet from there to the top."

"Sounds like it'll be a breeze!" Nora made a cynical face.

—

They dined in the restaurant, went to sleep before midnight, and got up again bright and early the next morning for a substantial breakfast that would give them the energy for the hike. The trail started out under a dense forest canopy, on a fairly warm day – for late November. Their spirits were high, but they did a total double-take when a turn in the trail brought them up behind some unexpected company. Amelia and Jack were already hiking up Mt. Pisgah, with Autumn, and – even more surprising – accompanied by another woman who also looked to be in her sixties.

"Phil! Nora! I never expected the newlyweds to be up this early!" Amelia teased.

"It was a last-minute decision," Nora looked at Phil with a smile. We're staying here at the Inn…."

"Great! This is my good friend from the university, Sister Evelyn. She's spending the weekend with us. Evelyn, this is the bride and groom whose wedding I told you about."

"I'm pleased to meet you two. Congratulations! You'll excuse me, though, if I don't interrupt my pace. See all y'all at the top!" And she was off…. Autumn was pulling on the leash in Jack's hand, anxious to follow Evelyn.

"We'd better be going, too," Jack laughed, "or she'll try to take off without us! See you up there."

Off they went at a slow jog, to catch up with Evelyn, and the newlyweds were alone once more. "That was startling!" Nora said, giving Phil a kiss. "But I guess if *they* can do it, so can we. Let's get going." Nothing like a little competition between generations to shake things up.

About halfway up the trail the path became steep and rocky, and they noticed that more and more hikers were turning around to go back down. Then they saw Amelia sitting on one of the occasional trailside benches, with Autumn at her feet. "Are you okay?" Nora sat down beside her.

"Yes, but my tendency to sprain an ankle made me decide to stop when it got so rocky. And Autumn was uneasy whenever we came upon an aggressive dog, so she's keeping me company here. Jack went on, so Evelyn wouldn't be alone up there. How are you two doing?"

"At our age, we don't dare complain," Phil said. "We'll see you on the way back down. I'm sure that Autumn will keep you safe."

—

Jack had caught up with Evelyn before they reached the summit, and they emerged into an open area at the top that was drenched in bright sunlight. The first thing that drew their attention was a communications tower – a necessary contraption in this day and age, but one that certainly spoiled the mood and the view.

They tried to ignore the tower, and gravitated instead toward a wooden observation deck where they had an exceptional view of the French Broad River Valley and the Blue Ridge Parkway. Nora and Phil soon joined them, and they enjoyed Sr. Evelyn's comments about the beauty of Western North Carolina. It sometimes takes an outsider to help you appreciate your own surroundings.

Amelia and Autumn were glad to see all of them on their way back down – especially Autumn, who loved attention from anyone who was willing to give it to her. She was a prime example of her breed, and seemed to know it. Amelia and Jack never came home without being greeted with licks and wags. They always described her as a dog who would alert them about strangers approaching the house with her fierce barking, but as soon as they were invited in she would morph into their best friend.

Amelia was happy to be reunited with her husband, and she used the opportunity to invite everyone to the fast-approaching Christmas Concert of the Asheville Choral Society. "I didn't want it to overshadow your wedding, Nora," she said, "but this will be a very exciting concert in early December, with a special international arrangement of 'The Twelve Days of Christmas.' You won't want to miss it! Tell Jeff and Eric that I can get tickets for everyone who wants to come! Jack, remind me to invite my choir members, and Annie, too."

"You'd better make a list, like Santa, and then check it twice!" Jack suggested.

When they all reached the trail head again, it was an unspoken agreement to let Nora and Phil get back to their honeymoon, alone. Everyone else peeled off to go home, including Autumn. She was blissfully unaware of anything special going on, and was only thinking about her own suppertime. "We could have dinner here at the Inn," Jack suggested.

"No!" Amelia countered. "Nora and Phil will probably dine here, and they want to be alone. Besides, we can't just leave Autumn in the car."

"It's a nice afternoon," Jack said. "Let's take the Parkway toward Asheville, and stop at the Tupelo Honey Restaurant on Hendersonville Road. They have outdoor seating, and Autumn could just curl up under the table while we eat. They serve those buttery southern biscuits and honey along with every order. That's something I'll miss if we ever move back up north."

"That and 'sweet tea.' If you order sweet iced tea anywhere else, even in Maryland, you get it unsweetened – with a couple of packets of sugar on the side. Not the same at all!" Amelia just shook her head.

Evelyn had to laugh. "It sounds like you two have turned into dyed-in-the-wool Southerners!"

15

"*You'll* come to the ACS Christmas Concert, won't you, Evelyn?" Amelia asked, as they drove back to West Asheville after their hike.

"I wouldn't miss it, if you don't mind my staying over."

"We never mind that, and Autumn loves it!" Jack confirmed.

Come to church with me tomorrow morning, Evelyn, and we'll tell the choir about it, too."

Annie was in her usual spot at church, more than halfway back. She liked to be inconspicuous, Amelia decided. Evelyn sat with the choir, singing her heart out, and Trish welcomed her enthusiastically. All of Amelia's favorite people were there – or almost all of them.

When the Mass ended and everyone was leaving, Amelia motioned to Annie to come up front where the choir sat. The group was starting to disperse, but Amelia asked them to stay a minute. "I want to invite all of you to the ACS Christmas Concert, the weekend of December 10. Come to the candlelight performance on Saturday evening, if you can, or else on Sunday afternoon. I have tickets to sell...."

"Hi, Amelia," Annie smiled. "I'll buy one for Saturday, and the Deerfield shuttle will bring me up."

That encouraged others, especially Trish and Evelyn, to buy tickets. Some people, like the choir director, wanted to come on Sunday because of other commitments. She had to cantor the Saturday evening vigil Mass every week. Nora called Amelia that night to order four tickets. Everyone was getting into the Christmas spirit, it seemed. "Jeff and Eric want to come on Saturday, too, Amelia. Isn't that super? I'll stop over some evening to pick them up – as soon as I get the money from them."

"Great! No rush, though. I'll set the tickets aside for the four of you, in case they sell out for that concert."

Before she knew it, Amelia was involved in dress rehearsals for the event – without their concert attire, however. Not that they showed up naked, but they weren't required to dress up before the first performance!

It was exhausting, though, standing on the risers for hours with only one ten-minute break midway through! When Amelia noticed that some of the singers had brought fold-up stools to sit on when they weren't actually singing, she decided to buy one, too. It fit easily on the risers, and made it bearable to wait around while the director ironed things out with members of the orchestra or the guy in charge of lighting.

—

At last, opening night arrived and the chorus sat upstairs in concert attire, going over their music binders as the audience began to filter into the church below. Jack and Evelyn had come early, with Amelia, and waited until the main church opened its doors to concert-goers. Evelyn wanted to sit toward the front, so she could see Amelia, but Jack always preferred the back. It was a guy thing, but he acquiesced because he had always liked Evelyn. Annie joined them, and then Trish – chattering with excitement and anticipation.

The stage curtains were uncharacteristically open, revealing the empty risers. Regular audience members knew that there was to be a procession at the beginning of the Christmas performance, and they shared this information with the West Asheville contingent when the four of them arrived. Now their group made up almost all of row seven, and they agreed on a plan to begin a rousing standing ovation when the director took her bow at the end.

The audience was already in a festive mood, while the chorus upstairs was comparing notes regarding some of the more difficult pieces. All at once the director breezed in, with just minutes to spare before concert time. She was elegantly dressed in black – velvet pants and jacket that would leave nobody wondering who was in charge. She was all business, and gestured for the chorus to rise for its warm-up. The women wore long black dresses with a strand of white pearls, and the men were in black tuxes with bow ties. It was quite a departure from the jeans and sweaters worn to weekly rehearsals, and the whole atmosphere was decidedly more formal.

They sang through the beginning of Thompson's <u>Alleluja</u>, just for luck, and then the director slipped out to take her place in the wings. Whispered reminders to "Break a vocal cord!" were passed along as the chorus formed two lines to walk downstairs. They each carried a small, unlit candle in a cardboard holder, and a black music binder. Each binder contained sheet music that had been lovingly and diligently annotated in pencil by its owner, to reflect the months of rehearsals leading up to each concert. The worst fate that could befall a chorister would be to lose or forget their priceless music binder, forcing them to use a spare set of unmarked music for the concert. It was the proverbial fate worse than death.

As the chorus waited in line in the hallway to process into the packed church, they lit each other's candles, and held their closed binders in the other hand.

They would have to sing the <u>Alleluja</u> from memory, since there wouldn't be enough light in the darkened church to see the music. Not to mention the impossibility of reading the music, singing, and walking at the same time, without tripping or bumping into the person ahead of you. As it was, walking with a lighted candle always caused the melted wax to drip and congeal on clothes and skin, and there was the ever-present danger of setting someone's long hair on fire by getting too close.

Amelia had worn her Christmas-tree earrings, of German Singing-Christmas-Tree notoriety, and checked with the woman behind her in line to make sure that the blinking tree lights were safely turned off this time. They were, although that person was curious to see them blinking, and Amelia turned one earring back on while they were waiting. Just then, the line began to move into the church, and she was juggling her lit candle and her binder, singing and walking – all the while trying to click off the battery on the back of her earring! When she turned to the woman behind her with a frantic question in her eyes, pointing her finger at the earring, the woman gave her a thumbs-up just before they entered the back of the church. That was close!

After they all took their places on the risers, they began the concert with an abrupt change of pace. They sang <u>The Twelve Days of Christmas</u>, with each of the days sung in the style of a different country's music and century – *a partridge in a pear tree* from 6th century Rome, to *twelve drummers drumming* from 19th century America.

It was a crowd-pleaser, composed by Craig Courtney – waking the audience up and thoroughly entertaining them. Evelyn loved the concert, Phil was a bit overwhelmed, and the rest of Amelia's friends fell somewhere in between, she later learned.

—

The show ended with a widespread standing ovation, started by Amelia's friends, and the usual bouquet of flowers for the music director. The chorus members made a beeline for their coats and/or purses upstairs, and Amelia graciously accepted the accolades of her family and friends afterwards. She couldn't have done it alone, of course. Everyone in the chorus was abuzz with talk of the after-party, which was to take place at a restaurant in downtown Asheville. The West Asheville contingent was all for it, being of a younger generation.

"I'm catching the shuttle back to Deerfield," Annie begged off, citing her beauty sleep before Mass the next morning. Trish had to work at the spa the next day, and Evelyn was, well, a nun.

"I'll take Evelyn back to our house, Amelia, if you want to go out with the kids" – meaning Nora, Phil, Jeff, and Eric. "They'll need a chorus member to get in, anyway."

"We'll drop Amelia off at your house," said Phil. "Don't worry – we'll take good care of her." Jack nodded his thanks, and everyone said goodnight.

The restaurant was rather small for that large a group, but Amelia and friends got in before they had to start turning people away. They formed one long table down the center of the dining room, which meant that you only got to talk to the people sitting near you. It was weird, but Phil *et al* really got into it, and everyone ordered drinks. Amelia missed Jack, and Nora finally noticed how quiet she was. "Do you want to go home, Amelia?"

"I *am* pretty tired. It's been a long night...."

"That's for sure. Why don't you finish your drink, and I'll drive you home. Phil can come back with Jeff and Eric later – I'm not hungry, anyway."

"You're a real friend, Nora. Thanks.... Tomorrow's another full day of singing – Mass, and then our second concert in the afternoon."

"You did great tonight, Amelia. It was an unforgettable concert. Drink up, and let's go.... Guys, Amelia and I are leaving. We're both tired. So, pick a designated driver to stop drinking *now*, and I'll see you later, Phil." She bent over to kiss him, and he pulled her down onto his lap.

"I love you, Nora," he whispered. "Can I bring you something to eat?"

"No, just get home safely, Phil. I love you, too."

"Bye, ladies," they all called out, as the server was taking their food orders.

Nora wasn't one for staying out late, either, so she didn't mind leaving. The highlight of the evening for her had been the concert, anyway. "So, how's married life?" Amelia asked, as they drove.

"So far, it's good! We're learning all sorts of things about each other that we didn't know when we were just dating."

"Like what?"

"Well, unlike Phil, I don't like late nights out. I guess I'm more of a homebody than he is. So it worked out well tonight. How about you and Jack?"

"He's definitely more social than I am, so it was nice of him to take Evelyn back early. We've been married long enough to adapt to each other that way, I guess."

—

Phil was having a good time, but he still felt odd about being out without his new bride. He texted her after a while. "Did you get home okay, baby?"

"Safe and sound, Sweetie! But I miss you…all alone here in our bed…."

"Let me see if I can light a fire under these guys. I'll get back as soon as I can."

"I'll be waiting...."

"Is Nora okay, Phil?" Jeff asked.

"Yeah. Just lonesome...."

"I know how she feels. When Eric and I had only been married for a few months and he had to stay late at school for a department meeting, I couldn't figure out what to do without him. The house seemed so empty, and quiet. It was unbearable, until he walked in the door with a pizza – and it wasn't just because of the pizza...."

"How would you guys feel about going home soon?" Phil asked. "I don't want to rush you or anything...."

"What do you think, Eric? Ready to hit the hay?"

"As long as *you'll* be there, I say let's go!"

16

Phil's phone rang in the middle of the night, that January. He always kept it handy, in case there were an emergency at the hotel that needed his attention, or something to do with Derek – God forbid! He picked it up quickly, hoping not to disturb Nora, but she was already stirring.

"Daddy? It's Derek – Momma's been in a car accident! I think it's bad...."

"Derek! Where *are* you?" Phil automatically hit speaker-phone so that Nora could hear, and he whispered to her, "Alicia – car accident!"

"I'm at the hospital where she works. I'm with Grandma and Grandpa...."

"What do the doctors say, Derek? Is she going to be okay?"

"They don't know yet—or if they do, they're not telling us…yet. I need you, Daddy! I'm so scared…!"

"Me, too, son…. Just hold on – I'll be there in half an hour, okay?"

"Okay, Daddy. Please hurry…!"

"I will, and I love you, Derek."

"I love you, too, Daddy…."

Nora was sitting up in bed, fully awake now. She thought immediately of the car accident years ago that had killed both of her parents…. Phil was almost dressed, and looking for his keys and wallet. "I'm coming with you, Phil!" she said. "Maybe I can help." She reached for her clothes, draped over a chair.

"Of course…thanks, Nora. Let's go…."

—

They drove in silence, until Phil just had to put his thoughts into words…. "Maybe she was driving home after a double shift. *You* used to do that sometimes, Nora…."

"Yes…it's tough when you're so tired. You just want to get home, and crawl into bed. We have to believe she'll be okay, Phil, for Derek's sake…."

"I'll try to believe…Derek would be devastated, if…."

"I hope you'll get to talk to her doctors, Phil. Hang on…we're almost there…."

Nora advised Phil to park near the emergency entrance to Haywood Regional Hospital, since Alicia might still be undergoing treatment there. When they walked in, it was a madhouse full of people waiting to be diagnosed, and relatives waiting for word on their loved ones. Phil spotted Derek and his grandparents at the far end of the waiting room, and Nora followed him over. Derek looked up as his father approached, and flew into his arms. "Daddy, you're here!"

"I'm right here, Derek, and everything's going to be okay now…." Phil wished he could believe that himself, as he looked over Derek's shoulder at Alicia's worried parents. "Mr. and Mrs. Stone…this is my wife, Nora. She's a nurse, too, and she wanted to come." They nodded, their minds preoccupied. "Can you tell me what happened, Mr. Stone?" Phil asked.

"The ambulance got called to the scene of the accident, between here and Alicia's house. I guess she was driving home after her shift, when a drunk driver blew through a stop sign and T-boned her car! That damned fool must have been flying, to have had such an impact on our baby girl! You can bet he's sitting in a jail cell already, or he should be…!"

"They're doing some kind of x-rays on her right now, Phil," Alicia's mother sobbed, "to see how bad her injuries are. We just have to wait…." He and Nora found seats nearby, and Derek stayed close to his father.

—

When the doctor came back out, he walked over to Alicia's parents and asked them to follow him. Phil jumped up, but then realized that he wasn't a blood relative, or even legally related to Alicia, so he sat back down. Alicia's mother said something to the doctor, who nodded, and she came over to get Derek. "The doctor said that you could come too," she said.

Phil and Nora watched them disappear from the crowded waiting room, and just sat – holding on to each other, but alone with their own thoughts. In Nora's experience as a nurse, if the news were hopeful the doctor would have said so before taking them back to their loved one. But who knew what this hospital's practices were, she thought. Before long, a nurse came out. "Mr. and Mrs. Clark?" she called out to the room, and they followed her down the hall and through the double doors. They passed numerous examining rooms, some with open doors while others were closed.

The nurse stopped at a closed door, and ushered them in.

Alicia lay motionless and partially covered on the examining table with her eyes closed…her family gathered around her, still in shock. "She's dead!" Derek ran to Phil in tears and drew him into the circle surrounding his mother. "I'm very sorry, Mr. Clark," the doctor repeated his findings, "but Ms. Stone has died of massive internal injuries sustained in the car accident she was involved in. We did everything we could to save her, but the force of the impact was much too strong, I'm afraid."

Alicia's father was irate! "What about the bastard who did this? I'd like to get my hands on him!"

"He was brought in with only minor injuries, so he was treated and taken into custody by the authorities. You can contact the Waynesville Police Department for any further information, Sir."

Despite her grief over the death of her only child, Alicia's mother knew that there were decisions that had to be made. "Is there a chaplain that could join us for a few minutes, Doctor? We need some guidance about what to do now, for our daughter…."

After the chaplain helped them contact a funeral home in the area, it was time to say the first of many goodbyes to a daughter, a mother, and a co-parent. It made sense for Alicia's parents to take Derek home and stay with him for a few nights in his own familiar surroundings.

They all lived in the same community and were thinking that, if Derek eventually moved in with *them*, he could keep going to the same school with his friends. One step at a time, though, and Phil reassured Derek that they would all see each other again soon…before they parted ways that day.

—

"Well, well…if it isn't Miss Alicia Stone, or at least her spirit." Phil's mother's spirit, Alice, welcomed her son's ex-girlfriend to heaven that same day. "Everyone always thought that *you* would end up marrying Phil, Alicia, just because your first name was so similar to mine, I guess."

"That just goes to show you how wrong people can be, doesn't it? And where would he be now, if he *had* married me? A widower with a teenaged son, that's where. He's better off with Nora, I think."

"I agree, but he still has a teenaged son! Where do you want Derek to live, now?"

"I have nothing to say about it anymore…."

"But if you did…?"

"Derek is an active kid – he has lots of friends, plays sports, is good with computers…. Frankly, I think my parents would have a hard time keeping up with him.

"He loves *Phil*, too, but it would be a big transition for Derek to move in with him and Nora. He'd have to leave his whole childhood behind. I think they'll let him decide, since he's old enough – almost fourteen – to make up his own mind."

"The law would be on Phil's side, as Derek's father, if he wanted to challenge your parents for custody."

"I don't think Phil would do that, Alice, if Derek wanted to stay in Waynesville with his grandparents."

"It's a tough decision to ask a kid to make, Alicia."

"Don't blame *me*! I didn't want to die this young, believe me…! That drunk came out of nowhere – *I* was the one who had the right-of-way!"

"Heaven is full of people like you who died too young, just going about their business…."

———

When Mr. and Mrs. Stone pulled up to Derek's house with him that afternoon, they were all totally wiped-out, physically and emotionally. The three of them walked into a house that was altogether familiar to them, and yet they saw it through different eyes now that Alicia was gone.

She had left her mark on everything she touched, from the fresh flowers on the kitchen table to her neatly-made bed. They were all still in a state of shock about what had just happened, and Derek went straight to his room and slammed the door. He obviously wanted to be left alone. His grandparents understood.

Mr. Stone opened the fridge, looking for something to eat, while his wife just stood staring at the multicolored hot-house chrysanthemums arranged in a vase. Suddenly the reality of her daughter's death enveloped her, and she collapsed onto a chair amid the first rush of tears that day. Her husband came to her, not knowing how to comfort her, and his own eyes teared up as he sat down next to her and took her hand. His wife, used to being the one who always found the bright side of every disaster, smiled through her tears. "At least now we know what kind of flowers she'd like for her funeral...."

"Don't cry, Momma," Alicia's spirit pleaded, knowing that she couldn't be heard. "Go and talk to Derek. He's mad at the world right now, but you could always talk *me* out of that mood. He needs you, Momma, more than ever."

Alicia's mother calmed down, and she suddenly felt the impulse to go and check on Derek. She glanced at her husband, and went to knock on her grandson's bedroom door. "Derek, it's Grandma. I need someone to talk to...."

The door slowly opened. "Can't you talk to Grandpa?"

"He doesn't like to talk about emotions," she smiled. "*You* know that. He just keeps it all inside, and thinks that everyone else should do the same. It would help me so much if I could talk to you, Derek. Please…?"

The door opened all the way, and Derek stood aside to let her in. His bed was a shambles, but he pulled out his desk chair for her. He closed up his laptop, and plopped down close to her. She knew that if she waited long enough, he would get tired of the silence and say something…. "Why did she have to die, Grandma? She didn't live nearly as long as you have…."

"If I could have taken her place, I would have gladly done that, Derek."

"I didn't mean that – I don't know *what* I meant! I'm just so confused!"

"Me, too. I think we might just have to add her death to the list of unsolved mysteries in this world of ours."

"You mean like why some people get cancer and some don't? Or why some people never find the right partner in life?"

"You mean your Momma, don't you, Derek."

"She dumped Daddy, but then he found Nora and Momma never found anyone else. Now she's gone...."

"But she had *you* all those years, honey. You were more important to her than anyone. She died as a happy mother, because of you. Not everyone is blessed with a child to love."

"You were, Grandma. But now she's not here for you anymore."

"But I still have *you* to love, Derek, and you still have me and Grandpa, and your Daddy. She would want us all to keep loving each other now, more than ever."

17

They all got through Alicia's funeral somehow. The only bright spot, that brought a smile to her mother's face in the midst of so much sadness, was the sight of so many beautiful chrysanthemums – at the funeral home, at the little church in Waynesville, and on her casket. Alicia's spirit was right there, of course, making sure that her son Derek was being taken care of properly. He was surrounded by the love of his father, his grandparents, and his other family members and friends. In fact, he was beginning to feel a bit smothered by everyone's attention.

Derek had moved in with his grandparents at their request, at least for now. His school routine remained the same, although his bus schedule changed slightly.

When spring break rolled around, Phil asked if he'd like to spend it in West Asheville with him and Nora, and Derek jumped at the chance to get away for several weeks from the constant reminders of his mother, provided by her parents. His grandparents agreed to let him go, as they continued to sift through the contents of Alicia's house alone, removing her personal belongings with an eye toward possibly renting the house at some point.

Evidently, Alicia had left her house to Derek in her will, to do with as he wished when he came of age. Until then, his grandparents finally decided to rent the furnished house, as a way of continuing to pay off the mortgage every month. Derek agreed to this arrangement, since it didn't require him to do anything or make any decisions about it right now. A fourteen-year-old boy had other things to occupy his mind – like school, and girls, and going to West Asheville for two whole weeks to stay with his father and Nora. Now it was up to them to rearrange their work schedules accordingly, however….

They staggered their days off so Derek wouldn't be completely alone – except on weekends, when the three of them did stuff together. It was fun for all of them, but it also made them realize that it wouldn't be feasible to have Derek with them full-time until the fall, when he would be starting high school. Derek understood their concerns, and was actually looking forward to spending the summer in Waynesville with his friends. Everything in life was a trade-off, he was learning, and so were his grandparents.

They treasured Derek's time with them, but they knew that the day would come when his father would want to claim the right to raise his son. It was only fair.

—

While Derek was at his father's house for spring break, Nora had taken a day off to spend with her stepson so that Phil could take care of some business at the hotel in Asheville. She was having coffee and doing dishes while she waited for Derek to wake up. In her mid-twenties, she was only about ten years older than he, and she could clearly remember sleeping late as a teenager, too. Somehow their growing bodies just needed more sleep than adults did. She was wondering what he might like to do today, but there was no sense deciding anything without his input. She could never predict the interests of a teenaged boy!

"Hey, Nora! Sorry I slept so late – I don't get much sleep on school days, so…."

"Probably because you stay up too late! No worries…I'm enjoying my day off. How about breakfast – I was just about to make some eggs."

"That sounds great! Make mine scrambled, and I'll do the toast. You know…my Momma was glad that you married my Daddy, Nora. She told me so. I guess she knew that it would never work out for the two of *them*, and she was right, because…"

"Sometimes things just work out the way they're supposed to, Derek, even if we don't understand why. I remember losing my own parents, and how hard that was. I was so proud of you when you read some lines from your Grandma Alice's journal at her funeral. I know that she was proud of you, too."

"She wanted us to celebrate her life, not mourn her death...."

"Your Momma would probably want you to feel the same way about *her*. She was an accomplished nurse, and helped a lot of people."

"Like you do, Nora."

"Oh, I'm just trying to follow in her footsteps.... Your Daddy told me that you have your Grandma Alice's journal now. That's a nice memento of her. Do you ever write in it yourself? That could be a way to remember things about your Momma, and honor her memory."

"I do like to carry it with me – I have it here...."

"Since you have some free time during these two weeks, why don't you put down your thoughts about your Momma? I think she'd like that. You know, she and your Grandma Alice are probably getting together in heaven right now – and talking about *you*!"

"Do you really believe that, Nora?"

"All I know for sure is that your Grandma Alice believed it, and that's good enough for me!"

—

"Any ideas what we could do today, Derek? Your Daddy won't be home until suppertime." Nora was drawing a blank.

"Not really…."

"Have you been to the Biltmore Estate?"

"Yeah… years ago. Daddy took me to see the mansion. That was pretty interesting, and then we went into the gift shop. He bought me something, but I can't remember what it was."

"Well, your Daddy and I have guest passes now, so we could get on the estate for free – as long as you pretend to be Phil Clark. What do you think?"

"That would be so cool, Nora! What else is there to do, besides the mansion?"

"We could have lunch in the Stable Café, that used to be a real horse stable, and then we could go to see the winery and take the winemaking tour. Our neighbor Jack works there."

"Let's do it! I bet none of my friends have been *there*!"

It felt like an undercover mission when they drove through the checkpoint at the gate. Nora presented her two guest passes, and the guard waved them through after a quick glance at Derek. There was no reason to think that he wasn't Phil Clark, or maybe the guard's mind was on his upcoming break. After passing through the ornate portal, they followed the road that wound slowly through the estate for fifteen minutes or so before reaching the parking lots. There were regular shuttle buses that transported guests to the mansion from that point.

It had apparently been George Vanderbilt's idea to build up the suspense in the minds of his personal guests, until the magnificent mansion finally came into view. It was built to resemble the French Palace of Versailles, which George had so admired on his many trips abroad. Rather than enter the mansion itself, Nora and Derek walked to the nearby Stable Café, passing the time in the gift shop until their table was ready for lunch. The café had preserved the look of the original stable, and many of the dining tables were nestled inside the former stalls. The menu was casual, but the soups and sandwiches were elegantly served…and priced.

Next on the agenda was the estate's winery, a short shuttle-ride away. As they proceeded to get in line for the tour, they spotted Jack Flynn working his magic – answering questions, cracking jokes – anything to keep people happy, so the time would seem to pass quickly for them as they waited. "Hi, Nora…hey, Derek! It's nice to see you two here!"

"Derek's on spring break, so we thought we'd do some sightseeing in town. He's never been here to the winery."

"This place is fascinating, Derek! It's a real behind-the-scenes tour of the winemaking process – while the vintners are actually working. If you want to try some different wines, Nora, go to the tasting room afterwards and Derek can enjoy some fresh grape juice instead. Come back when you're twenty-one, Derek, and we'll set you up with the real stuff, okay?" That brought a smile to his face.

"I might get Phil a bottle of wine before we leave, Jack, so he won't feel left out of our visit."

"I'll tell whoever is at the cash register to give you my 20% employee discount, Nora, so stock up."

"Thanks, Jack! We'll invite you and Amelia over to help us drink it."

—

Phil loved his three-bottle set of a white, a rosé, and a red Biltmore wine – all fairly dry, just the way he preferred them. Nora postponed inviting the Flynns over to share them, however, when she got a huge surprise sometime later. She was pregnant! "Which bottle should we open with dinner, Nora?" Phil had asked, when they were back to their usual routine after Derek left.

She had already had an inkling about the possibility, and a store-bought test had confirmed it that afternoon. "I won't be drinking wine for a while, Phil, but you go ahead and open whichever one you want."

He missed the cue, as many men would, but then caught on and just stared at her. "Nora…?"

"Yes…I just found out that we're expecting a baby together, Phil!"

"But…it seems like you only just stopped taking the pills!"

"In January, actually, before Alicia died. I guess that both events were just meant to be – something good to come after all that sadness…."

He held her close, being careful not to squeeze too hard…and she smiled at his protectiveness. "I thought that I could never love you more than I already do, Nora, but I was wrong. You've made me happier than I ever believed I could be! When…?"

"Sometime in October. I can't believe it myself!"

"Derek will have a little brother, or sister…. When can we find out…?"

"Not for several months yet. Patience, 'Daddy'…!"

"Can we at least tell everyone?"

"Let's wait another month, to be sure everything's in order, Phil…."

"You're the boss, 'Momma' Nora. How does it feel?"

"Like we've just been given the best gift that life has to offer."

"Our parents must be so proud! This baby will break the chain of lonely offspring without a sibling, in both our families – you, me, and Derek. He'll be so excited about the news! When can we tell him, Nora?"

"Let's at least wait until we see him in person! News like this deserves more than a text, or even a phone call."

There was no such thing as *waiting around* in heaven, however! Phil and Nora's happy news was the occasion for immediate and prolonged celebration among all four of their parents, and anyone else who might even remotely be interested. Jane and Robert Walker congratulated their friends, the Clarks, but couldn't help thinking about their own kids' lives. "I wish Lorraine and Karl would get busy, too!" Jane sighed.

"Even Jeff and Eric have options," Robert commented, "if they wanted to consider them."

18

It was another month before Derek was able to visit them again in West Asheville – what with baseball practices and his upcoming middle school graduation! It was already an exciting time for him, but Phil and Nora could hardly contain their own excitement about the news they had been trying very hard to keep a secret from everyone. By the end of her first trimester, they decided to tell Derek when he came, and include their closest neighbors by throwing a small party at their house. They made it another pot-luck dinner, so Nora wouldn't have to spend all day Saturday in the kitchen.

Now that Alicia was gone, Phil couldn't very well expect her parents to bring Derek to his house in West Asheville for a visit, so he drove over to Waynesville on Friday to pick him up. It was all he could do not to give away their secret, but he knew that Nora would be upset if he told Derek without her – and rightly so.

"What can we do this weekend, Daddy? It's supposed to rain tomorrow, all day…."

"Well, we can make popcorn and watch movies on TV, or play video games, but there'll be plenty of food for you to help us eat at dinnertime, Derek. Jeff & Eric, and Amelia & Jack are coming over for a pot-luck party."

"What's that?"

"Everybody brings whatever they want to contribute to the dinner, and we make something, too. Then we set it all out, and everyone helps themselves. We never know exactly what will be in the pots people bring, but it's always something good. We can help Nora by grocery shopping in the morning, and anything else she needs us to do."

"That'll be fun. Grandma and Grandpa never invite people over, so it's pretty boring at their house."

"I'm sure that they used to entertain when they were younger, but it gets harder the older you become."

"I hope I never get that old, then."

"You'll change your mind about that as the years go by, Derek…."

———

People and their pots started arriving by 6:00 Saturday afternoon, and the first were Jeff and Eric from next door. "It's raining cats and dogs out there, you guys! Here, this goes on a low burner until we're ready to eat." Eric carried in the heavy Dutch oven and plopped it down on the stove.

"It smells great!" Derek exclaimed. "What is it?"

"Eric whispered in his ear, "pork roast…."

"Mmm! What have *you* got, Jeff?"

"Mashed potatoes with sour cream and chives. It can go in the oven, just to keep warm. Don't tell anyone, Derek, but it's one of the few things I know how to make."

"We brought some wine, too, just because you can never have too much wine." Eric set the two bottles of red on the table, that was set for seven people.

"Amelia and Jack just pulled in the driveway," Nora called out from the kitchen. I don't blame them for driving, in this torrential downpour!"

They were laughing as they ran up on the porch with their arms full. "Whose idea was it to have a party in the middle of a flood?" Amelia handed off her bags and bundles to waiting hands.

"Maybe Noah?" Derek laughed, helping Jack with what he was carrying. "What did you guys bring?"

"I think it's a casserole of some sort – possibly corn?" Jack looked at Amelia, and she nodded. "And some wine – you can never have too much wine."

"I'll stick to the meat and potatoes," Derek said to Phil, under his breath.

"I've got the salad," Nora carried it in to the table, "and a surprise dessert!"

"Let's have a glass of wine, to warm us all up." Phil held up one of the bottles Nora had bought at the winery.

"I propose a toast, to friendship." Jeff raised his glass. "May we never be without it!"

Nora and Derek clinked their tall glasses of ginger ale together, as the others sipped their white wine. "Are you just keeping Derek company, Nora?" Amelia asked, noticing the difference in their glasses that the guys hadn't.

"No, it's just that I won't be drinking any wine for another six months or so," she smiled.

"Why?" Jeff asked, clueless.

"Because Phil and I are expecting a baby! We just found out recently, and we wanted all of you to know!" Nora hugged Derek, who looked like a deer caught in the headlights.

"It'll be a baby brother or sister for you, Derek!" Phil put his arm around his son, hoping he was as happy about it as they were....

"I hope it's a girl, Daddy. Then Nora won't be outnumbered anymore!" He smiled shyly, and Phil stopped holding his breath. It was going to be okay....

"This calls for another toast," Jack called out. "To Nora and Phil – nobody can keep a secret like they do! Congratulations!"

"So, what's the surprise dessert, Nora?" Eric raised an eyebrow. "Now that you're divulging secrets...."

"You'll find out when I serve it." She felt self-righteous, picturing her cherry dump-cake under wraps in the kitchen.

—

Jeff wasted no time in calling his younger sister Lorraine in Wilmington. He figured that Phil was too much of a gentleman to rub it in. He was right. "Hey, Lorraine. I have some news about our next-door neighbors."

"The honeymooners?   I hope they're not getting divorced already! They've only been married about six months…or maybe less."

"No…they're having a baby!   They just announced it."

"Oh. Well, that's quite the opposite, isn't it! Leave it to Phil to beat the rest of us to the finish line…."

"Is it a race? I didn't know that, Lorraine…."

"Never mind – I'll call him to congratulate them, of course…. I wonder if Nora blindsided him."

"That's beneath you, little sister."

"I know. I guess I'm just a sore loser."

"Since *you're* the one who turned down his indecent proposal, I'd say that you got what you wanted."

"You're right, as usual. I have no reason to complain. Thanks, Jeff. I'll give him a call…."

———

"Hi, Phil.   It's your friend on the Eastern Shore. Do you have time to talk?"

"Sure, Lorraine! It's nice to hear from you. What's up?"

"I've been remiss.... Jeff told me that Derek's mother Alicia died after Christmas, and I meant to give your family my condolences. How is Derek?"

"He took it pretty hard, especially since it was so unexpected, but he's living with Alicia's parents for the time being. He's finishing the school year in Waynesville, and then we'll see."

"He's lucky to still have *you*, Phil. You've always been a good father to him."

"Since you've been talking to Jeff, you probably know that I'll have another chance to prove myself in that department this fall. Nora and I are expecting a baby."

"Yes, he did tell me that. Congratulations, Phil, and to Nora, too. Your life seems to be taking shape by leaps and bounds. I'm happy for you."

"Thanks, Lorraine. How are you and Karl doing, if you don't mind my asking?"

"We're still seeing each other, if that's what you mean, but I have no news to rival yours. We seem to be taking it slow, or maybe it's just me that doesn't want to jump into anything. I'm not sure why."

"Sometimes in life you just have to take a chance, and see what happens.

"There aren't any guarantees, but I'm sure you know that. We were a prime example, weren't we? I loved you, but I still got my heart broken. I'm not sorry that we tried, though. You were worth it, Lorraine."

"Thanks, Phil. I'm not sorry, either, but I guess it just wasn't meant to be. Give Nora my best wishes, and Derek my condolences, too. I'll try to do better at keeping up with developments in West Asheville. When's the baby due?"

"October. Stop in to see us whenever you come home, and we'll introduce you to him, or her."

"I will, but that's just the thing, Phil. Wilmington is my home now, and that's not likely to change…."

———

In May, Nora's obstetrician at the hospital told her that the baby's gender would be visible on a sonogram, if they wanted to find out. Of course they did! She made an appointment for the two of them, and they were so excited that they couldn't sleep the night before. "Did you and Alicia find out about Derek before he was born, Phil?"

"No. We were so young, in college, and she was shocked just to find out that she was pregnant. Luckily, she didn't start to show until that semester was over.

"She took the fall semester off to deliver Derek, and then her parents took care of him when she went back to school after Christmas. She never could have gotten her nursing degree without their help. But she didn't want *me* in her life anymore – just Derek. I've supported him all these years, at least doing my share, and she never kept me from seeing him. I'm grateful to her for that, especially now that she's gone."

"Well, this baby is going to be raised by both its parents, all in the same house. We'll love him or her as much as we love each other, and Derek will know that we love *him*, too. Let's get some sleep if we can now. Tomorrow will be the big reveal…!"

Nora's doctor welcomed them into her examining room the next morning and everything was ready. They watched the screen, as the doctor moved her magic wand over Nora's baby bump, but Phil had no idea what he was looking at. Nora did, though, and when the baby turned slightly toward them it was perfectly obvious to both doctor and patient. "It's a girl, Phil! We're having a baby girl! Derek will be so happy, and so am I!"

"That makes three of us, Nora! Our very own little daughter – just imagine! I wish my mother were here – and your mother, too! Maybe they knew about it even before *we* did, though. I'd like to think so…."

They left the doctor's office, way up on cloud nine, and stopped for lunch downtown.

This was an occasion that needed to be savored. "I can't even have a drink to celebrate, Phil! Let's talk about names for our daughter, instead. Our mothers are both gone, so maybe we could honor them by using their names."

"You know that my mother's name was Alice, but what was *your* mother's name?"

"It was Mary…."

"How about Mary Alice Clark? That has a nice ring to it. What do you think, Nora?"

"Only if we actually call her Mary Alice, to honor them both at once. Agreed?"

"Done! And when she grows up, maybe her friends will call her Mac…."

"Did you hear that, Mary?" Alice's spirit was full of pride. "They're having a baby girl, and they're going to call her Mary Alice."

"Just so her nickname isn't *Mac*! That sounds like a takeoff on 'Mac the Knife'!"

19

Phil and Nora converted their small guest room into a nursery over the summer, and helped Derek redecorate Phil's former bedroom as his own. They told him that he could make the move from Waynesville to West Asheville anytime it felt right to him. He was reluctant to leave his grandparents, of course, but even they had begun to realize that it was time. They were ready for a more sedate way of life, and Derek was excited about starting high school in Buncombe County in the fall. He would have to leave his good friends behind, but he wouldn't ever forget them.

Phil looked in on Derek in his new digs one weekend when he was visiting. It looked like a totally different room. They had repainted, re-carpeted, and rearranged the furniture. Derek had made it his own with posters of his sports and celebrity idols, and little-league baseball trophies to remind him of his friends.

"Ready to move in, Derek? This room never looked so good when it was mine. Your Grandma Alice was constantly after me to pick up my clothes, and take my dirty dishes down to the kitchen."

"It probably won't look much different than that after *I* move in, either, Daddy. I guess I take after you. Momma used to close the door to my room, when she didn't want to see what it looked like…. It helped avoid arguments, I think."

"You really miss your Momma, don't you, Derek?" Phil sat down on the chair next to his desk. Derek had been lounging on his bed, phone in hand, but sat up before answering.

"It's just that everything changed after she died. Someone else is renting our house now, and I went to live with Grandma and Grandpa. Now I'm moving again, to live here. I'm not sure where *home* is anymore."

"Maybe home isn't a place. Maybe it's wherever your loved ones live. That's why we want you here with us, Derek. We love you, and we want this to be your home, too."

"I love you and Nora, too, Daddy, and baby Mary Alice when she comes. But I feel sad to leave Momma and her parents behind in Waynesville."

"We'll take you back to see them whenever you want to, Derek.

"We can all visit your Momma's grave together, too, and take her flowers. Let's do that when we pick up all your stuff, as soon as you're ready, okay?"

"Thanks, Daddy. Maybe the next time you come to get me. I need to talk to Grandma and Grandpa first, and make sure they're okay with it. I'll let you know…."

———

When Derek wasn't visiting them, Nora and Phil worked on the nursery every weekend – ordering furniture, stenciling murals, and stocking the changing table with essentials. Even though Nora was a first-time mother-to-be, her nurses' training helped her know what to expect and how to prepare. Sometimes she and Phil would just sit in the nursery together, she in the rocker and Phil on the floor by her side, taking in the magical atmosphere they had created with all their hard work and feeling a sense of satisfaction. They were proud of themselves. "I might go part-time at the hospital when Derek moves in, Phil, just to be here to make him feel welcome."

"And to take it a little easier than you have been…. That's a good idea. How much maternity leave do you get after Mary Alice's birth?"

"Six weeks of paid leave, and six more weeks of unpaid leave if I need it. That would take me through Christmas, if necessary.

"Then I'd like to start back part-time at first, if that's okay with you."

"Whatever you need or want is just fine with me, Nora. I never got to be a part of Derek's early years, so I want to make up for that with our daughter."

"Thanks for being so flexible, honey. You're the best husband and father I could ever imagine!"

"Not everyone was willing to give me that chance...."

"Then it was their loss, and my gain."

———

Derek talked to his grandparents about him moving to West Asheville, and by August the plans were made. Phil showed up in Waynesville on the appointed weekend, and he was nervous. He didn't know Alicia's parents very well, and he wasn't sure how they felt about Derek leaving. Maybe they were heart-broken, but didn't think they had a choice. Phil was Derek's father, after all. He knocked on the door of the small house, as he had done ever since Alicia died. Only, this time he wasn't just picking Derek up for the weekend – he was taking their grandson away for good.

Mr. Stone appeared at the door, and welcomed him in. Derek ran down the stairs to hug his father.

"Grandma's in the kitchen fixing us all some lunch before we leave, Daddy. She insisted." Derek led his father into the large eat-in kitchen to say hello.

Mrs. Stone, how nice of you to invite me for lunch. I hope you aren't going to any trouble."

"Not at all, Phil. It's just a pot of homemade chicken noodle soup and some grilled cheese sandwiches. Derek likes that for lunch on Saturdays, so that's what we have when he's here. Just so you know…."

This was going to be harder than he thought…. "Come and sit down here, Daddy. Grandma likes us to eat our soup while she grills the sandwiches. Then they're nice and crispy for us."

"I brought you some flowers, Mrs. Stone, and a bouquet for Alicia, too. I thought we could stop by the cemetery after lunch – so I can pay my respects."

"That's very kind of you, Phil. I'd like that. Now sit down and eat your soup while it's hot…."

It was a quiet lunch. No one had much to say except a quick "congratulations" in passing, in recognition of Phil and Nora's happy baby-news. Mr. Stone offered to help Derek bring his belongings downstairs, while his wife finished her lunch and had a chance to talk to Phil alone.

"Derek has been a blessing to us, Phil," she said, "and I thank you for letting him stay so long with us. But now it's time for him to join your growing family, and take his rightful place with *you*. There's something that I want to give you...."

She reached into a folder on the kitchen counter, and handed Phil a piece of paper. It was Derek's original birth certificate, listing Philip Clark as his birth father. You and Derek should have this now, as proof of your relationship, and whatever else you need it for.... And there's one more thing that my husband and I would like you to know, Phil. If Derek ever wants to change his surname from Stone to Clark, that would be perfectly all right with us. He'll always be our grandson, regardless of his name, and all we want is for him to be happy."

"Thank you so much for your generosity, Mrs. Stone...and your love for Derek. He loves you both very much, too."

Derek's stuff was piled up by the front door – in boxes, several old suitcases of Alicia's, and various bags. It seemed like a lot for a fourteen-year-old, until Phil remembered that it constituted all of his son's worldly possessions. "Let's pack the car, Derek," Phil said, and then we'll follow your grandparents over to the cemetery. I have the flowers for your Momma in the car, too."

—

Alicia was buried in the same cemetery where her parents would someday be laid to rest, and their two burial plots were nearby hers. The foursome walked over to the spot together, and Derek placed the bouquet of his mother's favorite chrysanthemums on her tombstone while saying a prayer that his Grandma Alice had taught him. Alicia's spirit heard her son's heartfelt prayer, and wished she could just hold him one more time. Phil put his arm around Derek instead, and promised Alicia that he would take good care of their son for as long as he lived. She couldn't ask any more of him than that....

Mr. and Mrs. Stone came closer then and offered their own silent prayers for their daughter, who was taken from them in the prime of her life. They too believed the old adage that there was nothing more agonizing for parents than losing their child to a premature death.

"Ready to go, Derek?" Phil whispered, and his son looked up and smiled. Phil noticed that they were almost the same height now, and it made him feel old somehow – but proud at the same time. "We'll be out to visit all three of you again soon." Phil gave each of Derek's grandparents a hug. "Thank you for taking such good care of Derek, just as you did of Alicia. She was an excellent mother, too, and a good person...."

Then it was Derek's turn, and tears come to his eyes as he realized what this goodbye really meant. It was a turning point in his young life.

"I love you two so much," he sobbed, hugging them both together. "You're the next best thing to having my Momma still here. Thank you...."

"I hope you'll let us know how you like your new school, Derek." Mrs. Stone put on a smile for his sake, and her own. "My love goes with you...."

"We wish you all the best, Derek." Mr. Stone remained stoical, to keep from breaking down. "And we love you very much...always. Now I think we'll stay here a while, and talk to your Momma...."

Derek looked back and waved as he and Phil walked to their car. Mrs. Stone was still watching him go, and she waved, too.

—

Derek was greeted by a sign over the front door, as they pulled in the driveway: WELCOME HOME, DEREK! He was pleased, but embarrassed that everyone in the neighborhood would see it. That was ridiculous, he told himself. Surely all their neighbors already knew that he was moving in. As soon as he walked in the door with an armful of boxes, however, it became abundantly clear – the whole neighborhood was *there* to welcome him! Phil relieved him of the boxes so he could greet everyone...some of whom he barely knew...but the house was full of people, good will, and laughter.

"We thought you'd *never* get here!" Nora smiled, and hugged him.

"It was hard to leave them," he admitted.

"I'm sure," she agreed…but then she took him by the hand into the dining room, where the table was laden with every kind of finger food imaginable. "Look what everyone brought, Derek! They're so happy that you'll be part of our neighborhood now, and offers of part-time jobs have been pouring in for you – lawn work, babysitting, snow shoveling in the winter…if we should be lucky enough to get snow! After you get something to eat, you can cut your cake. That was *my* contribution." There it stood at the end of the table – a chocolate layer cake with the same message on top: WELCOME HOME, DEREK! He was overwhelmed!

Derek knew that his family loved him, but to find out that he had a ready-made circle of friends and neighbors here in West Asheville was more than he could ever have dreamed possible. Jeff and Eric were there, of course, and Amelia was pleasantly surprised that she and Jack were included, too. They lived several blocks away, but they had been through a lot with Nora and Phil since their recent arrival in North Carolina – both good times and bad – and they wanted to be a part of their new friends' lives. When someone started singing "For He's a Jolly Good Fellow," everyone steered Derek over to the cake, and Nora gave him a knife to cut it.

"Want some help with that?" A young man volunteered to take over, so Derek could get a bite of his own cake.

"I'm Rob, and my Dad's a pastry chef, so…. Nora said you'll be a freshman at the high school this fall – so will I."

"Cool. I'm Derek, but I guess that's obvious. Will you be taking the bus, Rob…?"

20

Once the welcome-home party was over and the revelers collected their empty platters and went home, Derek was finally able to settle into his room upstairs. Not that he unpacked everything that night, but he knew that it would all be there for him to see the next morning when he woke up in his new bed…in his new room. He had been sad to leave his mother and his grandparents, but it seemed like he was starting a new life that day – one that would see him into adulthood, and one that was meant to be. He felt more in control than ever and, most important of all, he felt like he belonged in this new little family of his.

Nora and Phil had Sunday off, and they all needed a break…especially Derek. It had been a non-stop weekend so far. "Finding a place for everything?" Phil asked, hearing Derek banging around in his room mid-morning. He and Nora had long ago finished breakfast.

"Hi, Daddy. I think so. It's a lot more room than I had at Grandma and Grandpa's…. Can I ask you something?"

"Of course, son…anything."

"Can I start calling you Dad, instead of Daddy? That's what Rob called his father last night, at the party. It just sounds a little more…I don't know…grown-up."

"For me, or for you?" Phil laughed. His son was definitely growing up before his eyes. "You can call me anything but Phil – I draw the line at that!"

"Thanks, Dad…. Rob will be starting high school in the fall, too. He seems like an okay kid – at least he knows how to cut a cake!"

"I'm glad you got to talk to him. His family lives just down the block – good people. He's a big brother, too!"

"Cool. Maybe I can get some pointers."

———

Derek took breaks on Sunday, for breakfast and lunch, but otherwise he holed up in his room – shelving books, deciding which clothes to hang up and which to just shove in a drawer in his chest, and basically trying to convince himself that this room was all his for as long as he wanted it to be.

Of course, Derek had felt the same way about his little room at his mother's house, but that hadn't lasted forever. What if something happened to his Dad, too? Would they have to move to a smaller place? Maybe he wasn't really safe, after all.

"You look like you're lost in thought, Derek," Nora commented, from the open doorway to his room.

"I was just thinking that all this seems too good to be true – for me, I mean."

"It's as true as it *can* be in this crazy world, Derek, and there's no one who deserves it more than you do. You've been shuttled around a lot for a boy your age, but now you're here to stay. I promise…."

"But what if something happens to my father? What if I lose him, too?"

"He's pretty tough, but there are some things that we have no control over. So, then it would just be you and me…and Mary Alice. But we three would still be a family, Derek. That wouldn't change. We would support each other, just like we do now, because that's what families do. Now that you're here with us, I've changed to a part-time schedule at the hospital until the baby is born. She could come any time now, so I want to be well-rested and ready."

"You can't fool me, Nora! It has something to do with *me*, too, doesn't it?"

"I cannot tell a lie…I can't wait for an excuse to go shopping with you for school clothes, and baby clothes for Mary Alice, too! Will you come?"

"I'd better, or you might buy me something dopey for the first day of school, and I'd *never* make any friends!"

"Then let's go soon, so you don't have to worry about that! How about tomorrow?"

"It's a date – no, forget I said that! I just heard someone on TV say it…in an old sitcom. Tomorrow would be great. Thanks, Nora."

—

Phil had left Nora alone to talk to Derek. He knew it was important for her to establish her own relationship with his son, apart from him. But he was longing to talk to him too, now that Derek was here for good. Their time together had only ever been two nights in a row, every fourth weekend or so. Now they had all the time in the world, by comparison. "When you get tired of sorting through your stuff, Derek, let's go for a walk. It's not that hot today…."

"Okay, Dad. When I get to the bottom of this box, I'll come and find you. Where will you be?"

"In the garage, puttering…." *It must be a guy thing.* Derek wouldn't worry his father about his fears, though. It was bad enough that he had mentioned them to Nora.

"So, here you are, Dad! Let's walk.... I haven't been getting much exercise since baseball season ended. How about you?"

"It's times like these when I wish we had a dog to walk three times a day. Then we'd all get some regular exercise! One new family member at a time, though. We're growing by leaps and bounds – you were the first, soon Mary Alice will be here, and then maybe we'll think about a pet. I want to tell you about a conversation I had with your Grandma before we left their house, though, Derek. She gave me the original certificate of your birth, from fourteen years ago."

"Where did she get *that*?"

"Probably by going through your mother's important paperwork after she died. Your Grandma knew that I would need it to register you for school here, since my name is listed there as your birth father. But there was something else she wanted to talk to me about. She thought that the time might come when you would want to change your last name from Stone to Clark, like mine."

"But my name has always been the same as Momma's, and my grandparents'."

"And that was reasonable, since you were in their custody until now. But I want you here with us for always, Derek, and I'm your father.

"If you ever decide that you want to change your name, your grandparents wanted us to know that it was perfectly all right with them. You'll always be their grandson, no matter what your name is, and all they want is for you to be happy. Just think about it, Derek. We can do the paperwork together anytime you want, or not at all. It's your decision, and I'm okay with whatever you decide, too."

—

Derek had a vivid dream that night. He was introducing himself to his new classmates at school, and after saying his first name he stopped…. He didn't know what his last name was – Stone or Clark. Everyone started laughing at him for being so stupid, and he turned and ran out of his homeroom. He ended up in the parking lot, and saw his mother's car parked there. She was waiting for him behind the wheel, and smiled when he approached. "I thought you were dead!" he gasped.

"I am, Derek, but my spirit returned to give you some advice. Are you ready to hear it?"

"Oh, yes, Momma! What should I do about my name…?"

"I think it's time for you to have your father's name, Derek. My parents and I are your past, but your father is your future. Become part of his family by becoming Derek Clark, and you'll all be glad you did. I'll always love you…whatever you do."

Alicia and her car both disappeared from sight, and Derek found himself alone in his bed. He went back to sleep but when he awoke the next morning, it was perfectly clear to him what he should do. He found his father and Nora having coffee together in the living room. "I dreamed about my Momma last night, Dad, and she encouraged me to change my name to Clark. I think it's the right thing to do, too."

"If you're sure, Derek, come to work with me this morning in Asheville. We'll do the paperwork at City Hall at lunchtime, and when it takes effect I can register you for school as Derek Clark. Then we'll all have the same name."

"But Nora was going to take me shopping for school clothes today, Dad."

"Don't worry, Derek," Nora said. "We can go shopping tomorrow. I'm not scheduled at the hospital until Wednesday. Go with your Dad and take care of business first – that's more important…."

"Thanks, Nora. I can't believe I get to do things with both of you here! It's really like a dream come true."

"Eat something first, Derek," Phil said, "and then jump in the shower. We have to leave in half an hour."

"Things happen a lot faster here than at Grandma and Grandpa's house, Dad. I like that!"

———

Everything went like clockwork in Asheville, and Derek even got to see his father at work at the hotel for the first time. He and Rob got together on the days that Nora had to work at the hospital, and Derek had a chance to get to know him better. They even took the same bus on the first day of high school, and he was proud of the clothes Nora had bought him. It seemed like his life was starting to fall into place at last, but there were more surprises to come when they got to school. He and Rob were in different homerooms, since Rob's last name came toward the end of the alphabet, and now Derek's was more toward the beginning.

When Derek found Room 120, there was a temporary sign by the door that read "Mr. Walker's homeroom." He knew that he was in the right place, but what was his neighbor Jeff doing at the teacher's desk? He stopped dead in his tracks. "Hey, Derek! Come on in. I didn't even know that you were in my homeroom until I checked the list last night. I guess we both changed our names, right? You're Derek Clark, and I'm Mr. Walker. But what's in a name, anyway? 'A rose by any other name would smell as sweet....' Never mind – occupational hazard. Take a seat, Derek. Welcome!"

At least Jeff was just as nice being Derek's homeroom teacher as he was as their neighbor. He wasn't taking English Literature…yet, so he didn't have to worry about flunking Jeff's class…yet. When he walked into geometry class, though, there was Eric – Jeff's husband – handing out questionnaires as the teacher! It was weird, but oddly comforting, to see them both here in such a different setting. His father must have known – that Derek would be bumping into the two of them at school, if not working with them this closely!

Derek and Rob had the same time slot for lunch, so they were able to sit together and compare notes. Rob knew lots of the kids there, having grown up in West Asheville, and he introduced Derek around. This was going to be a whole new ballgame compared to middle school, in more ways than one. First of all, the girls were cuter – and, well…older. Were they thinking the same about him? He was playing it cool, though, and acting like he had better things to do than hang out in the cafeteria. Actually, he did.

He had seen the baseball-trophy display case in the hallway, and got to the gym early for phys-ed class. The instructor was a guy about his father's age, and seemed approachable. "Hi, I'm Derek Clark. I'm in your next class, and I was wondering if there will be tryouts for the baseball team."

"Have you played before?"

"Yes, in middle school…in Waynesville."

"Well, this is football season coming up, Derek," he said, with a smile, "but hold that thought until early spring, and we'll see what you can do…."

21

Mary Alice Clark wasn't due to be born until mid-October, but her impatient parents started to get edgy as soon as it was no longer September. Nora was still dragging herself to work at the hospital several times a week, but her heart wasn't in it. She'd much rather be sitting in her rocker in the nursery, looking at the baby-animal murals they had stenciled or, better still, rocking her newborn baby girl. Phil's nervousness stemmed more from the uncertainty of getting Nora to the hospital in time. This wasn't his first child, but he hadn't been as much involved in Derek's birth as he would be in Mary Alice's.

Derek himself was more concerned right now with school and just being a teenager, than he was with the imminent birth of his half-sister. He trusted his Dad and Nora to do what needed to be done to present Mary Alice to the world, and to let him know if they needed his help.

So it came as a shock to him, and to Nora, when she began having stomach pains while eating a take-out burger at home with Derek in early October. Sometimes she just craved a greasy burger-with-the-works in the late afternoon, and Derek would call for delivery when he got home from school. It was something they had bonded over during her pregnancy, since teenagers are always hungry and Phil sometimes got home late from work.

"Do *you* feel any stomach discomfort, Derek?" she asked, putting down her half-eaten burger, and trying the fries instead.

"Nope, nothing unusual."

Nora took a deep breath, and then another bite out of her sandwich. "I feel better now. Maybe it's the onions, but they never affected me like this before…. So, how did your math test go today, Derek?"

"Not bad. At least I don't *think* I failed! Eric always tells us what to study, so there aren't any sur…Nora! Are you okay? Should I call Dad?"

"No, just some more pain. I don't think I'll eat any more of that burger, though." She glanced at her watch. "This can't be labor yet – all my friends say that first babies are always late, and this is two weeks *early*! Talk to me, Derek, and let's see if the pain comes back…."

"Uh…Rob told me that he's going to take Spanish next year, since we have such a large Hispanic population in the Asheville area. Do you think I should study Spanish, too?"

"Well, what other languages are offered? You should definitely choose one, but only if the language itself interests you…Oh…Derek! Here it comes again – and only five minutes from the last one! This isn't just indigestion! Call your father – if he isn't almost home already, we'll ask someone from around here to take us in. Here's my phone…."

"Dad, Nora's in labor, and her pains are five minutes apart! Are you on the way home?"

"No, I haven't left Asheville yet! Call 911, or maybe Amelia and Jack are at home. I'll leave now, and meet you at the hospital! Don't worry – it'll be fine…!"

—

"Should I call Amelia and Jack, Nora? Dad's still in Asheville!"

"Yes, they're in my phone's contact list. Ask them to come right over, if they can. My case is already packed – by the door."

"Amelia? It's Derek. Nora is in labor, and Dad's still at work. Can you take us to the hospital?"

"Oh, my God! Yes – we'll be right over, Derek!"

"They're coming, Nora! What do you need?"

"Just your help getting out to their car, and grab my case and my purse by the door! Thank God you were here, Derek!"

Amelia and Jack jumped in their car and drove right over. Nora leaned on Derek, and Jack stashed her case in the trunk. She lay down in the back seat with her head in Derek's lap, and he quietly reassured her during the twenty-minute drive to the emergency room. Her contractions were coming every four minutes now, and Jack pulled right up to the door and ran in to get a wheelchair. An attendant came out pushing a chair, and helped her into it. "Are you a relative?" he asked Derek.

"Yes, I'm her step-son," he answered proudly.

"Then come in with us and fill out her paperwork, while I take her back to the examining room. You'll have to park your car, Sir," he said to Jack, "if you want to wait."

"We'll see you inside, Derek," Amelia said, deciding for both of them.

Derek approached the desk, as Nora disappeared down a hallway with a quick wave to let him know she would be okay.

He was very glad to be able to give his name as Derek Clark to the receptionist as the one registering his step-mother, Nora Clark. He really *was* a member of her family! Then all he could do was take a seat. Amelia and Jack came running in, bringing Nora's case and purse. "They might need her identity and insurance cards at the desk, Derek," Amelia said, holding Nora's purse.

"Could *you* take them up, Amelia?" Derek asked. He was feeling totally overwhelmed all of a sudden.

"Of course, and we'll hold onto her case and purse until your Dad gets here. She won't need them right now, anyway.... She's in good hands, Derek, and they know her here. She'll get first-class treatment, that's for sure."

—

Phil came rushing in a minute later, and went straight to the desk when he saw Amelia there. "They took her into an examining room, Phil," Amelia said, so happy that he was there.

"I'm Nora Clark's husband, Philip Clark," he told the receptionist. "Can you find out where she is now? She's in labor!"

"Just a moment, Mr. Clark. I'll call...."

Phil turned to Amelia. "I can't believe this is actually happening now, Amelia! Thanks so much for bringing her in this quickly."

"Jack and Derek and I are all here, Phil. Where else would we be, at such an important time?"

"Mr. Clark, your wife was taken up to the delivery room, in the maternity ward…second floor. There's a waiting room up there, as you might imagine."

"Thank you. We'll go up, but I don't think we'll be waiting very long. At least I hope not."

"I'll call ahead and let them know you'll be there, in case of updates."

"Let's collect the others, Phil. Oh, here comes Derek!"

"Dad! You're here!" He barreled into Phil's arms, a huge sense of relief on his face. Amelia went to get Jack, and Nora's case, *which was getting a lot of attention lately….*

"We're all going upstairs to wait, Derek," Phil told him. "Nora's in the delivery room already."

"Is that good, Dad?"

"It *is* a good sign that Mary Alice is ready to be born, son."

They reached the waiting room upstairs, but there was no doctor or nurse in sight…even in the hallway. The room itself was curiously empty, too. Maybe most babies were born during the wee hours of the morning. There was a coffee machine, probably for husbands who were trying to stay awake all night, but the four of them didn't need coffee. They needed information, and reassurance. Another man came in and sat down, too preoccupied with his own concerns to want to talk, as were they. Then a nurse breezed in, and they all looked up. "Mr. Clark?" she asked everyone, scanning the room.

Phil stood up, preparing himself for whatever she might say. "Would you come with me, Sir? The doctor would like to speak to you." Phil looked solemnly at the others, and left with the nurse. She led him down the hall to the open door of an office and motioned for him to go in, closing the door behind him and disappearing down the hall.

"I'm Dr. Farrell, Mr. Clark. Please sit down. Your wife's obstetrician was not on duty when she came into the ER tonight, so I'm acting in her stead. Mrs. Clark was almost fully dilated when she arrived, and there wasn't even time to prep her for the birth. My team went into action and I delivered your baby girl almost immediately. I'm happy to say that your wife and your new daughter are both doing well. Congratulations!" Phil had been expecting the worst, and now his relief was quite apparent. He dropped his head into his hands, and was unable to speak….

"Would you like to see them in the recovery room, Mr. Clark? We'll keep them both for several nights, while we perform certain tests on the baby and monitor your wife's overall recovery."

"Yes! Of course I want to see them, Doctor! Thank you!" Dr. Farrell called for the nurse to come back in.

"I need a minute to tell my son and my friends in the waiting room first. They have her suitcase and purse, too." *Why is the damned case so important…?* the doctor wondered.

"Certainly, but a change of clothes for herself and the baby are all she'll need when she's discharged. You should take her purse home, for safekeeping." The nurse knocked and came in, giving Nora's rings and her watch to Phil to take home, too. "Mr. Clark wants to make a stop at the waiting room first, Miss Perez. Oh, and Mr. Clark…a word of advice. If you and your wife ever decide to have another baby, she'll need to come in at the first sign of a contraction. She delivered after only an hour of labor this time. The next baby will come even faster – and if she tries for a third one, she would probably do well to spend the last two weeks of her pregnancy in the hospital. She would never make it in here in time, otherwise!"

"Thank you, Doctor. I'll let her know…." The nurse walked back down to the waiting room with Phil, and waited politely outside the door for him.

"She's had the baby, and they're both fine!" he announced to everyone at once. Even the other man, who was still waiting, congratulated Phil. "I can go in to see them now, but they'll be here for several nights!" He was so excited, he could barely contain himself. "I'll give the nurse her case, but you should keep her purse for her, Amelia – for safekeeping, the doctor said." *The blasted case and purse take center stage again....*

"Dad, could I go with you to see them?" Derek asked, hesitantly.

"Let's ask the nurse outside, Derek.... My son wants to see his step-mother and baby sister with me, if that's allowed." *Phil gave her Nora's case, as a peace offering. Phew!*

"I'll tell them I okayed it, Mr. Clark, since you won't be able to stay long, anyway," the nurse said. "We're moving her over to a private room down the hall after that."

"You two should go home, Amelia, and I'll bring Derek back with me. I can't thank you enough for being there for Nora and Derek tonight. What you did must be the very definition of what friends are for, or at least it should be. You'll get to see them soon, I promise." There were hugs all around, and then Phil and Derek followed the nurse to the recovery room. Several other women who had just given birth were also on hospital beds separated by curtains, for privacy.

The babies were in the nursery for the time being, unless they were being fed by their mothers. The nurse pulled back a curtain and there was Nora…her eyes closed, and dozing. "Hey, beautiful!" Phil whispered, and Derek hung back behind him. "I hear you're a new Momma, and I want to be the first in your family to congratulate you!" He leaned over and kissed her softly. "And I brought someone else with me, who insisted on being the second. Phil stepped aside to let Derek come forward and take her hand.

"My hero!" she smiled, and squeezed his hand tightly. "*She's* beautiful, too, Phil. Have you seen her? She's our own little cherub. Ask the nurse if she'll bring her in…."

"It isn't time for her to be fed again yet," said the duty nurse, "but I'll sneak her in for you to take a peek, Mr. Clark. When we move you to your own room tonight, Mrs. Clark, you can have Mary Alice right there with you, in her crib." The nurse brought her in and she was cozy and snug in her receiving blanket, wearing a little knit cap to keep her curly head warm. Phil held her tenderly for a few minutes, noticing her plump cheeks. She really did look like a cherub! Derek was afraid to ask if he could hold her, but Phil knew that he wanted to. He showed him how to support her head, and then passed her over to her big brother. Nora watched with pride as her menfolk handled the baby so lovingly, and she realized that Mary Alice already had them all totally wrapped around her tiny finger….

Thank You for Being a Friend

Thank you for being a friend
Traveled down a road and back again
Your heart is true, you're a pal and a confidant

I'm not ashamed to say
I hope it always will stay this way
My hat is off,
Won't you stand up and take a bow

And if you threw a party
Invited everyone you knew
Well, you would see
The biggest gift would be from me
And the card attached would say
Thank you for being a friend

And when we both get older
With walking canes and hair of gray
Have no fear, even though it's hard to hear
I will stand real close and say
Thank you for being a friend

And when we die and float away
Into the night, the Milky Way
You'll hear me call as we ascend
I'll see you there, then once again
Thank you for being a friend.

Andrew Gold (1978)

Susan Larmon (susanlarmon@yahoo.com)

Published works:

Fiction

- -**Time Travel 101** (a trilogy: **Swan Songs, Spy Songs,** and **War Songs**)
- -*Vive Les Vacances!* (a trilogy: **Total Immersion, Russian Roulette,** and **Father to Son**)
- -**Ellie's Opal**
- -**Memorial Service & Being a Friend**
- -**Spy Girl** (a double trilogy: **Spy Girl, Sheer Pretense, Collision Course, The Jasmine Connection, Practice to Deceive,** and **Danaë**)
- -*Ciao,* **Bella!** (a trilogy: *Ciao,* **Bella!, Never Did Run Smooth,** and **A Tangled Web**)
- -**Fireworks in Quebec & Body and Soul**
- -**Cinderella Summer** (a trilogy: **Cinderella Summer, Cinderella Rewind,** and **Cinderella Fast-Forward**)
- -**Nadia's Quest & Jeremie's Dilemma**
- -**Up In Smoke & Back Down To Earth**
- -**Death in Tahiti (Never As It Seems, Root Of All Evil, Tramps Like Us,** and **Olivia Takes Wing**)
- -**Front Window** (a trilogy: **Front Window, That's Amore,** and **Ratsstube**)
- -**Second Chances & Love of My Life**

Non-Fiction

- -**The Carpe Diem Kid**
- -**The Wiesbaden Years: Through Rose-Colored Glasses**
- -**Golden-Age Reflections**
- -**Prompt Me!**
- -**Moments in Time**

For Children

- -**Right on Time**

Susan Larmon (susanlarmon@yahoo.com)
Published works:

Fiction

-**Time Travel 101** (a trilogy: **Swan Songs, Spy Songs,** and **War Songs**)

-*Vive Les Vacances!* (a trilogy: **Total Immersion, Russian Roulette,** and **Father to Son**)

-**Ellie's Opal**

-**Memorial Service & Being a Friend**

-**Spy Girl** (a double trilogy: **Spy Girl, Sheer Pretense, Collision Course, The Jasmine Connection, Practice to Deceive,** and **Danaë**)

-*Ciao,* **Bella!** (a trilogy: *Ciao,* **Bella!,** **Never Did Run Smooth,** and **A Tangled Web**)

-**Fireworks in Quebec & Body and Soul**

-**Cinderella Summer** (a trilogy: **Cinderella Summer, Cinderella Rewind,** and **Cinderella Fast-Forward**)

-**Nadia's Quest & Jeremie's Dilemma**

-**Up In Smoke & Back Down To Earth**

-**Death in Tahiti (Never As It Seems, Root Of All Evil, Tramps Like Us,** and **Olivia Takes Wing**)

-**Front Window** (a trilogy: **Front Window, That's Amore,** and **Ratsstube**)

-**Second Chances & Love of My Life**

Non-Fiction

-**The Carpe Diem Kid**

-**The Wiesbaden Years: Through Rose-Colored Glasses**

-**Golden-Age Reflections**

-**Prompt Me!**

-**Moments in Time**

For Children

-**Right on Time**

<u>*Acknowledgements*</u>

The author wishes to thank:
      Carol Loughridge and **Susan Milligan**
         for their invaluable editing skills.

<u>*Bibliography*</u>

-"What's in a name? That which we call a rose, by
   any other name would smell as sweet."
      -from **Romeo and Juliet**
      -by Willian Shakespeare
      -spoken by Juliet in Act 2, Scene 2

-**Alleluja** (Randall Thompson)
      -one of the most widely performed pieces of
American choral music
      -first performed in 1940 at the Berkshire
Music Center

-**The Twelve Days of Christmas** (ar.Craig Courtney)
      -Thought to be French in origin, the verse was
published without music in England in 1780.
      -The tune we all know appears to have
originated around the turn of the 20th century.

-**Thank You for Being a Friend** (Andrew Gold)
      -Cynthia Fee sang it as the theme song for the
NBC sitcom **The Golden Girls**.
      -Betty White, who died in 2021 at the age of
99, was the last living star of the show.

www.ingramcontent.com/pod-product-compliance
Lightning Source LLC
Chambersburg PA
CBHW071412150726
48000CB00001B/275